CRAZY FOR YOU

Crazy for You

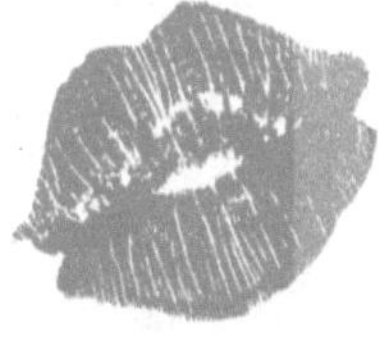

JILLIAN DODD

Editor: Jovana Shirley, Unforeseen Editing,
www.unforeseenediting.com

Jillian Dodd Inc.
Seminole, FL

ISBN: 978-1-962549-39-4

BOOKS BY JILLIAN DODD

Eastbrooke Academy®
Best Friends Aren't Forever
Popularity Isn't Easy
Kisses Don't Stay Secret
First Loves Are Hard To Forget

London Prep®
The Exchange
The Boys' Club
The Kiss
The Key
The Party
The Country House
The Choice
The Club
The Match

The Keatyn Chronicles®
Stalk Me
Kiss Me
Date Me
Love Me
Adore Me
Hate Me
Get Me
Fame
Power
Money
Sex
Love
A Very Keatyn Christmas
Keatyn Unscripted
Aiden

That Boy®
That Boy
That Wedding
That Baby
That Love
That Ring
That Summer
That Promise
That Forever
That Crush
That Girl
That Someday

Dating in the City
Writing Mr. Right
Heart Stopper
Crazy For You
Catching Feelings
Party of One
Save the Date
Urban Cowboy
Check, Please!
Happily Ever Afters

Crawford Brothers
Vegas Love
Broken Love
Fake Love

Spy Girl®
The Prince
The Eagle
The Society
The Valiant
The Dauntless
The Phoenix
The Echelon

Girl off the Grid

Chapter One

"WHAT DO YOU think?" I fling back the dressing room curtain, stepping out with my arms stretched to either side with a very serious, striking look on my face. Or so I tell myself.

I'm feeling dramatic.

Hayley, my best friend and toughest critic—the combination of which makes her the perfect shopping partner—tips her blonde head to one side, and her smooth forehead isn't so smooth anymore. "I mean, if you like it …"

So much for striking. "Oh, come on!" I groan, slumping. I'm not proud to admit it, but I might stomp my foot once or twice. It's all a frustrated, exhausted blur.

Okay, maybe *exhausted* isn't the right word. But I sure feel exhausted after going through the arduous task of shopping for Halloween costumes. As in actual, physical shopping. In a store. With doors and mirrors and people and cash registers. All of it.

For somebody whose entire life generally consists of online shopping, this is a pretty big deal. I even packed snacks in my purse, the way people do for toddlers when they know the kid will get hungry and cranky halfway through a trip.

Hayley waves a hand in my general direction. "I mean, it's cute, but don't you think it's a little young for you? You're twenty-five years old, Kitty, and you're gorgeous and successful. Why are you dressing up like some sort of cartoon character?"

I turn around to look at myself in the mirror beyond the curtained partition. "I don't look like a cartoon character."

"You're dressed like a superhero. Not even a cool superhero."

I run a hand over my breastplate—plastic instead of metal, of course. I flutter my bright red cape. "I don't know. I think I look powerful. Like a kick-ass general or warrior. Who happens to wear a cape."

"Either way, it's not doing anything for you. Try on that slinky black dress. I'm telling you, that's the winner."

Yes, and it happens to be the costume Hayley picked out for me. What a coincidence.

"Exactly who am I dressing up as when I wear that dress?"

"What does it matter? You dress up as somebody or something when you're a kid. When you get older, the entire point is to look sexy and enticing."

I shoot her a look over my shoulder, rolling my eyes. "Isn't that a little cliché?"

"Put on the damn dress, so I can look at you. Maybe we'll pick out a wig for you too. You can lose some of your inhibitions and pretend to be, I don't know, a witch or something. A sexy witch."

I have to step into the dressing room and close the curtain before the look on my face gives away just how tired I am of this whole misadventure. I love Hayley, I do, but she's forever trying to tell me how to live my life. Granted, most of the time, I need all the help I can get, but today, she feels impossible to deal with.

"I don't see why I have to go to this party in the first place," I grumble while removing my cape. "I won't know anybody there but you."

"That's exactly why you should go! How do you expect to meet interesting, new men if you keep crawling back into your cave?"

"It's called working," I mumble while removing my breastplate.

"Don't get all semantical on me," Hayley warns. "You know what I mean. It's like you only come out when you have to. I admit, you're doing better, but I still think you need more life, period."

"Gee, I thought I already had a life. What do you call dating two different men in just a few months?"

"I call it progress, but I'd still like to see you live a little. Do things you want to do but outside your apartment. Meeting me for drinks is not enough."

I take a long look at myself in the mirror. I'm in

my underwear, my long brown hair pulled back in a ponytail. My blue eyes reflect a little bit of the doubt Hayley's words have stirred in me.

Is she right? Probably. She usually is. It's always easier for us to have opinions about the lives of other people, isn't it? We can generally see the truth with no problem because we have the benefit of seeing the big picture.

It's the same for us when the tables are turned too. I can always tell when Hayley is working too hard, not taking care of herself. When you're the one in the trenches, battling it out, it's tough to pick up your head and look around and see things the way they really are.

Which is why I put on the stupid dress—because I want to fit in at the party. It's not for another three weeks, hosted by Hayley's firm. They rented out an entire swanky restaurant on the riverfront and even plan to have a yacht to take people out on the water. Just what that has to do with Halloween, I have no idea, but it sounds like it could be fun.

Normally, I would spend Halloween on the couch, eating Chinese takeout.

But when Hayley is on a mission, the girl is unstoppable. She's determined to get me out of my comfort zone and to challenge me by insisting I go to this party with her.

I guess I can't complain. If it wasn't for Hayley pushing me to do things I wouldn't normally do, I never would have dated a billionaire boss and a hot, sexy doctor, all thanks to her electronic spinner. I have to say, I might not have liked the idea at first to help my floundering book sales, but now, it has its benefits. I've managed to write a pair of books, which have been wildly successful so far. My doctor book just came out this week after being rushed through by the publisher, and all signs point to it selling really well. Much better than my last sweet romance, for sure.

Lesson learned. Even if I don't always agree with Hayley's methods, she's usually right in the end.

Just like she's right about this dress. It's tight, hugging all my curves, floor-length but with a slit on the side that just about reaches my hip. There's a waist-cincher sort of thing that goes over the top, meant to look like a corset but much more forgiving.

"Let me see!" Hayley's voice carries all the excitement of a little kid waiting to go downstairs on Christmas morning.

Darn it, why does she always have to be right?

For a second, I consider not showing her at all and letting my appearance at the party come as a surprise. Call it my perverse need to be stubborn. But I hate that know-it-all look she gets on her face.

I take my time in opening the curtain, and I don't make a big, dramatic thing about it like I did in my superhero costume. "Here you go," I sigh, shrugging. Bracing myself for what I know is coming.

And my beloved Hayley does not disappoint. First, her jaw hits the floor, just before her eyes almost bulge clear out of their sockets. "Oh. My. God."

My skin feels twitchy and itchy all of a sudden. "Don't," I warn, looking away. "You know how I feel about getting too much attention."

"No way, hon. You are way too hot in that dress to expect me to pretend like you don't look incredible. See? I told you!"

"One of these days, I'm going to keep count of how long it takes you to say *I told you so*."

"It's not like I don't give you plenty of opportunities to keep track." She winks before jumping to her feet to get a full look at me. "Turn around," she murmurs, moving her finger in a circle.

I do as she asked with a huff.

"I feel like a teenager whose mom insists on embarrassing them," I whisper, looking around.

She's making a little bit of a scene here, and we've attracted attention from a few shoppers.

"You're acting like one too," she sighs, handing me a protein bar. "Here. Replenish."

Not just yet though. I take a look at myself again, chewing my lip. "Do you really think I look all right?"

"Um, hell yes." She stands behind me, hands on my shoulders. "You're a beautiful, successful, stinking hot woman."

"Stinking hot?" I snicker.

"There's a reason you're the writer. Don't change the subject." Her hands tighten on my shoulders, and I manage to wipe the smirk off my face. "You need to own who you are. Sometimes, that means forcing yourself outside your comfort zone, but it's always for the best. No more hiding behind a laptop or an apartment door. There's more to life than work."

Okay, now, I can't help myself. "Look who's talking!" I laugh, turning to face her.

"That's different. And notice how every spare minute I have is spent doing things not involving work. Like this, today. Shopping with my best friend. Like the Halloween party coming up at the end of the month. I know it's easy to fall into habits, but it can be dangerous. You're in the middle of creating a habit, young lady. You don't want to become a recluse."

"Hardly." I go back into the dressing room and close the curtain to take off the dress, which of course, I'm going to buy because I'm not a complete idiot. I can be stubborn, but I'm not going to cut off my nose to spite my face.

"Yes, you are. You've barely come out with me since you and Jake ended things."

"Hello, I was on a deadline."

"That was weeks ago, and you haven't started your new book yet. You haven't even chosen the next trope. Don't think your little excuses are going to get you anywhere. I know you too well."

I swear, I don't even need to see her face to know how she looks. Smug, in case you're wondering.

I peek out from behind the curtain. "Let me guess. That's what today is really all about. You want to force me into choosing my next trope. May I remind you that's what I call work, and this is supposed to be free time."

"Fine, I'll let you off on a technicality, but you know the stakes here as well as I do. Ideally, you should get at least one more book written this year, if not two. I know it's a lot to ask in three months, but that's what the publisher wants. You told me so yourself the last time we got together, which was … what, after you submitted the final edited draft of the doctor book? It's been how many weeks since then? I'm pretty sure it was still summer."

She's right. I know I'm dragging my feet, just like I take my time getting out of my costume. I'm feeling a little burned out, point-blank, and the idea of finding and dating yet another type of man is even more exhausting than shopping in person for a Halloween costume.

"Why don't you choose one for me?" I suggest while pulling on the clothes I came in wearing.

Fall is probably my favorite time of year. I live for sweaters, boots, scarves, and pumpkins. Pumpkin pie. Pumpkin ravioli. Pumpkin muffins.

I really need to eat something. My protein bar is waiting, and I scarf it down in a few bites. Shopping is hard work.

"It just so happens, I've brought your handy-dandy trope-picker with me," she sings out.

"What a big surprise." I open the curtain, the dress over one arm and my purse over the other. "Yes, why don't you choose this time? Maybe you'll have better luck than I've been having lately—and I know, I know, I'm not supposed to get serious about the guys I'm dating."

The fact is, I've never been able to understand anyone who can date casually for more than a short period of time. I guess I form attachments quickly, which is unfortunate in a case like this, where I need to get in and get out of these relationships so I can churn out these books.

"You know I've been dying to do this, right?" She grins, sitting in one of the stuffed armchairs lined up in front of the dressing rooms. Seats for men I bet, where they can rest and wonder why they bother coming out shopping with their wife or girlfriend or daughter.

I sit next to her, my heart in my throat. "So long as you don't land on Santa."

"What is your big problem with sexy Santa? Good grief. I think you need counseling. Did Santa hurt you? Did you not get what you wanted for Christmas?"

"Spin the darn thing already," I sigh.

She does. We watch as options scroll past on the little screen, slowing, slowing …

Hayley lets out a tiny squeal. "Rock star!"

"Oh, help me." I groan loudly, sliding down in the chair until I fully resemble a toddler gearing up for a tantrum. "Why, God? Why?"

"Come on! It'll be fun!"

"Just where in the heck am I supposed to find a rock star to date?" I ask, staring at the ceiling. "I mean, I can't walk down to D'Agostino and pick one up."

"Leave it to me." She grins, standing. "Come on. I want some actual lunch before I have to go home and read a bunch of briefs."

"On a Saturday?" I hold out a hand, and she pulls me to my feet.

A rock star. Where the heck am I supposed to find one of those?

"Don't look at me that way. You know I'm always working—like you don't work on weekends." She hustles me over to the register like some chattering blonde-haired fairy godmother.

I'm shocked she lets me pay for the stupid costume myself and doesn't pull the wallet out of my purse on my behalf.

She's probably worried that if she leaves me to my own devices, I won't buy the costume. She's too stinking smart.

We're out of the store and on our way to grab a bite—yes, I know I just ate a protein bar, but come on, it was the size of my thumb—when I remember what she said before helping me up. "What do you mean, leave it to you?"

At first, all I get in response is one of her patented killer smiles. "Girl, you know I've got connections."

"In the music business? Last time I checked, you were working in a law firm."

"Duh. We have plenty of agents on the client list—and their clients too. Entertainment people. Actors, writers, musicians. Get it?" I'm surprised she doesn't knock on my head with her knuckles.

"Oh. So, what? You're going to have your boss hook me up with somebody? Doesn't that seem unprofessional?"

She huffs out a big sigh.

"I mean it."

"Leave it to me," she insists. "I'm telling you, I have my ways. You might be surprised at just how many hardworking lawyers and paralegals would jump at the chance to say they had a hand in the creation of a best-selling romance novel. Heck, there're a few lawyers in the firm who write under pen names on the side."

"No kidding?" I gasp.

"No kidding. Where they find the time, I have no idea. Anyway, lots of them know who you are and what you mean to me, and they'll be glad to help. I'll send up a signal on Monday. We'll see what comes of it."

I can't help myself. "Thank you," I cry, throwing my arms around her in the middle of the sidewalk, stopping us both in our tracks. "I love you."

"I know."

"I couldn't do any of this without you."

"I know that too." She laughs. "Come on, you dork. I'm starving."

"This is why I packed snacks." For once, I was the one thinking ahead.

"Yeah, but you're not the one who has to put up with you while shopping. Forget snacks. I'll need wine to get me through it next time."

"YOU KNOW, PRETTY soon, we're not going to be able to do this anymore. It'll be too cold up here." Matt takes a pull from his bottle of beer, smacking his lips. "I do like autumn beers. This pumpkin ale is pretty good."

"And you thought I was an idiot for buying it," I remind him with a roll of my eyes. "It doesn't taste like pumpkin pie at all, does it?"

"What can I say? I hear pumpkin, I think pumpkin pie. Who doesn't?"

"Most of the world, I guess." I can't help but feel just a little bit smug since Matt likes to make fun of me at pretty much every opportunity. For once, I'm the one making him feel like a dope.

"Anyway, I don't think we're going to have many of these warm days." He stretches his legs out with a sigh.

Warm is right. After a few days of temperatures being down in the fifties—which, at this time of year, feels pretty cold—today, it feels like spring. "I hope we don't have many more." I shrug.

He puts a hand to his chest, gasping. "Is that an

insult? You don't want to meet up on the roof?"

He is insufferable.

"This may come as a surprise, but not everything is about you. Shocking, I know. What I meant was, I like fall. I like feeling cozy and wearing big, thick sweaters and boots and jeans and scarves and hats."

"And lions and tigers and bears—"

"Shut up."

"And pumpkin spice lattes and pumpkin cereal and pumpkin beer."

"Last time I checked, that's your second pumpkin beer, and unless you want to pay me for it, you can keep your snide comments to yourself."

"It was your turn to buy the beer."

"That doesn't mean I can't demand repayment when you insist on being such a tool."

He winces. "Tool? Now, I know you're irritated since you don't usually go any more extreme than *jerk* or *dork*."

"Yeah, well, I'm growing as a person. Expanding my vocabulary. You know, it's not a good idea for a writer to become complacent with their vocabulary."

He winks, and I know the direction his thoughts have taken the second a slow, knowing smile starts to spread. "That's true. You've definitely been expanding your vocabulary, if what we first talked about was the sort of stuff you were writing."

"The stuff we first talked about?"

He slaps his forehead. "Oh, right. You were half out of your mind on tequila shots. Let me remind you. You had me read part of what you'd tried to write, and it was … not good."

"I do remember that, thank you very much."

He snorts. "What did you call it? *Her silky petals*?"

"Do you ever get tired of being you?"

"Not yet." He shrugs with a grin. "And now that we're on the subject, who's your next victim—I mean, boyfriend?"

I hold up one finger. "For starters, none of these guys are my boyfriend. We date, yes, but they are not boyfriends. You need to keep that one in mind."

"Noted." He nods.

He's trying to keep a straight face, which I guess is something I should be grateful for, but I wish he didn't always have the impulse to laugh at me in the first place.

I hold up a second finger. "Two, dispense with the whole victim thing. They are not victims. They are human beings who are fortunate enough to spend time with me."

"It sounds like you've been reading girl-power self-help books."

"So what if I have? Which I have not, by the way," I add when it looks like he's about to laugh. "But you have to admit, I'm sort of a big deal. The total package."

"That's Hayley talking." He snickers before

taking another drink.

Darn him. "So what? She's right. What's wrong with being confident? And with people like you in my life, who always make fun of me, it's a good thing I do have some self-confidence."

"Then, why do you hang around me?"

"Geography, nothing more. You just happen to live across the hall."

He holds his hand to his heart. "You sure know how to put a man in his place. And here I was, thinking you liked the company."

I do sort of like the company. I can't let him know that though. It doesn't take much for things to go to his head, and he already has a monstrous ego.

"Hey, I call it like I see it."

"In all seriousness, you're pretty hard on yourself."

"Thanks," I mutter, rolling my eyes.

"See? How am I supposed to try and help you when you get all … that way?" He waves his hand in my general direction.

"For one thing, I didn't ask you for help. So, your opinion isn't exactly needed. And like I said, you're the one always being so hard on me."

"You know I'm kidding, right?"

I lower my brow. "All the time?"

"Most of the time?" he counters with a wince. "Some of the time?"

"I thought so," I sigh.

"Lighten up!" He laughs, going for another beer.

"Listen, I joke around because it's fun to joke around with you. Maybe because you take things so seriously. I don't know. Or maybe I'm really a mean person."

"That sounds about right."

"What can I say?" He runs a hand through his brown hair, making it stand up on end. "That's how I am. Ask my sister. I teased her when we were kids to the point where she would cry."

"Are you bragging? Because it sort of sounds like you're bragging a little bit."

"No! I'm just saying, I joke around a lot with the people I like."

He likes me, does he?

"So, you teased your sister just because you liked her?"

"And it was fun—don't forget that part." When I roll my eyes, he adds, "But yeah, I don't waste my time teasing anybody I don't care about. I guess, in a way, you're like my surrogate sister. You live right across the hall, just like she did when we were kids, and you're always getting yourself into situations that I would swear couldn't be for real. Like, how does anybody light their sleeve on fire during dinner?"

"How many times do I have to tell you? My sleeve was a little puffy, and the stinking candle was right in the middle of the table!" Like I did it on purpose or something. "Trust me, that was one of the most humiliating experiences I've ever been through. It's not like I go around experimenting, seeing how much I can embarrass myself today."

"I don't think you could do a much better job of it if you tried on purpose."

"Why do I even bother with you?"

He's still laughing when he leans a little closer, arching an eyebrow. "You didn't tell me. Who is it this time? What's your trope?"

Terrific. I should've had more to drink to brace myself for what's coming next. He'll never stop asking if I don't tell him since he'll know I'm holding back for a reason. I might as well get it over with.

"A rock star."

The fact that he's silent for so long is actually kind of alarming.

"What's the matter? Did I break your brain?" I ask in a whisper. "Do you smell burned toast?"

He shakes his head, nostrils flaring. His lips are pressed together, and there's a flush creeping up over his cheeks. He's practically turning purple.

I lean back in my chair, deflating. "Go on. Let it out before you die from trying to hold it in."

The first tiny snort escapes. Then, the second. Before long, he's doing that laugh of his, and I'm sitting with my head in my hands.

"A rock star?" That's all he can manage in the middle of so much laughter at my expense.

"Obviously, it doesn't have to be an actual rock star," I add while he's laughing. "A musician should do the trick. But somebody with a following, somebody with fans and gigs or whatever they're called."

"Oh, so you're not going to show up at the next big concert at Madison Square Garden and throw your underwear on the stage?"

"I like to do that anyway," I retort, sticking my tongue out at him. "No, that's not what I'm going to do. Jeez."

"No, I guess not." He wipes his eyes because, of course, he's still crying with laughter. "No, you need something more immediate than that."

"This is why I didn't want to tell you. Because you always take things too far."

"You know how funny I think this is in general. Why do you act surprised when I laugh?"

"I guess, deep down in the bottom of my heart, I hope, this time, you'll have grown up a little bit. What can I say? I'm an optimist."

"You should know better by now." He grins. "I'm pretty much a preteen boy when it comes to my sense of humor."

He leans forward, elbows on his knees. He's in his uniform of a T-shirt and jeans, his feet bare, as usual. I wonder what he'll do once the weather turns colder and he has no choice but to wear shoes if he comes up here.

"Seriously though, how do you plan on meeting this guy?"

"Hayley says she has connections at her law

firm. Lawyers who represent entertainment agents—that sort of thing."

He blows out what sounds like an impressed whistle. "Nice to have friends in high places."

"In situations like this, yes, it is nice. Because you know me. I wouldn't have the first clue how to go about this. I never have the first clue how to go about anything when it comes to this. It's still so far outside my wheelhouse—this concept of dating somebody to get inspiration for my books."

"This is the third one. It must be getting at least a little easier by now, right?"

"Not really. Like you said, I take things seriously, and it's more for work than my own fun."

"Yet you seem to keep attracting these guys, right? I mean, you managed to hook your first two guys without too much trouble."

I won't say what immediately comes to mind because I know it's wrong. I know I'm not supposed to form deep connections to these men, that I'm only dating them for the sake of my work.

But after not being enough for not one, but two men in six months, well, my pride stings a little. A lot actually. Who could blame me for being gun shy? Who could blame me for wondering if I'm the problem, not the perfect-on-paper men I keep finding?

Matt knows how I feel about this since I cried to him about it. I really wish I hadn't. He doesn't need to know those intimate details of my life. Besides, he's got a life of his own. I should know. I'm the one who ends up having to listen to the screaming and moaning through the wall we share.

Which is why, instead of complaining to him like I would to Hayley—who is so tired of it, I'm sure—I force a smile. "That's true. But I've gotten lucky. They landed right in my lap."

"And now, you have a best friend with the ability to hook you up with a candidate for your next dating project. I mean, you practically live a charmed life. I hope you know that."

"I wouldn't go that far." I snort before finishing off my one and only beer.

I never drink too much when we sit up here together, mostly because I don't trust myself. I'll end up saying something stupid again, like I always do when I get drunk. And in spite of the girls' nights I have with Hayley, I'm still a lightweight. I only drink maybe once a week, if that.

"I would. I know you're being modest because you're not a stupid person. You see things the way they are. And you know as well as I do that you've been crazy fortunate in your life. A great career, a great apartment, and you live across the hall from me, which pretty much means you hit the lottery."

"I would definitely not go that far," I mutter.

He ignores this. "You'll find a way to make good on this. I'm sure you will. You always do. Some people are skilled at landing in a pile of shit and coming out, smelling like roses."

"Are you sure you've never considered a career as a writer? Because you have such a way with words."

Chapter Three

911. Girls night. No excuses.

Hayley's text is probably the only thing that could get me up and out of the apartment in record time—looking pretty decent, I might add. She didn't order me to look hot, which tells me this is a serious situation.

I can't help but worry as I hurry my way to our normal spot—a trendy restaurant and bar a few blocks from my apartment. It's only Monday night—two days after she promised to spread the word at work. *What if she got in trouble for that? Darn it, that's probably it.*

I'm all apologies the second I find her seated at a high-top table near the bar. She must've just gotten here because, otherwise, she would be swarmed with interested men by now.

"I'm sorry, I'm so sorry! It's all my fault. Is there anything I can do to make things right? Oh my gosh. This is so awful."

Hayley just sits there, staring at me. "Do you need medication? I'm starting to think you need medication to manage your brain."

It's my turn to stare at her. "I thought something had gone wrong today, and why you called this emergency girls' night."

"Yes, on the emergency girls' night, but nothing went wrong."

I have to hold on to the table when my legs almost go out from under me. "Jeez Louise! What is wrong with you? You could've at least told me everything was okay when you texted. But no, I've been worried sick about you for the past half hour. I was worried you'd gotten in trouble for asking around, the way you'd said you would."

"For heaven's sake. Sit down, take a few breaths. I already ordered drinks and appetizers."

It's not until I sit and calm down enough to really pay attention to her that it's clear she's practically vibrating. I don't think I've ever seen her this way in all the years we've known each other.

"What the heck happened? Did you get a promotion? I mean, you deserve it."

She shakes her head, eyes sparkling with some hidden excitement. "You're never going to believe this."

Now, my blood is starting to hum too. "Tell me already! You're driving me crazy!"

She leans in, cheeks now flushed. "Okay, get this," she says with an urgency in her voice that I'm not used to hearing from her. It's like she went back in time ten years and is about to tell me she just got invited to the prom by the captain of the football team. "As it turns out, one of the firm's partners does handle an entertainment agent whose client just so happens to be launching a tour of small venues around the city, starting this weekend. As in four days from now."

My eyes widen. Maybe Matt's right about the whole *charmed life* thing. "Really? That's convenient! And small venues mean I'll have a better chance of actually making contact with him. Who is it?"

"Guess." Now, she's bouncing up and down a little bit.

"I literally have no idea. Who can make you react like this?"

"I'll give you a hint." Her eyes narrow, her smile widening. She's practically lighting up the whole room. "We both love him."

"We both love a lot of people. That doesn't help all that much."

"We both loved him when we were teenagers."

Hmm. Intriguing. "That explains why you're acting like one right now."

"Focus!" she barks, drawing a different sort of attention than she's used to.

For once, people are frowning in her direction instead of in mine.

"Okay. Somebody we both loved when we were teenagers. So, like, before we met?"

"Yeah, way before that. But we have him in common."

Who the heck could she possibly be talking about?

Maybe I need to open up my mind a little more because every name that comes into my brain is immediately rejected. It couldn't possibly be this person or that person—but it has to be one of them, right?

I'm trying to narrow it down and think of who she could mean when she blurts it out, "Dustin Grant!"

And then the room goes dark for a second, and I might or might not black out. It's all a blur, caused by the fact that my brain has melted and is running out of my ears.

When I finally come out of my stupor—which might've lasted three seconds or three hours for all I know—I manage to find my voice. "Dustin. Grant. *The* Dustin Grant? Dustin Grant, who, for most of my adolescence, was the man I pictured marrying? Dustin Grant, whose babies I wanted to have by the dozen? Dustin Grant, who was the reason I wrote Kitty Grant all over every notebook and folder I owned?"

"Dustin Grant, whose face was all over my sheet sets. Remember I told you about how I made my parents buy me three separate, full sets of sheets with the band's pictures on them just so I never had to go without Dustin's face on my pillowcase when I went to sleep? That Dustin Grant."

I have to hold my head in my hands since it might fall off otherwise. "Oh my God. I can't breathe. Dustin Grant. He ushered me into womanhood, Hayley."

"And so many others." She giggles. "I knew you would freak!"

"So, what? He's trying to revive his career? Crazy 4 You broke up years ago."

They were the biggest band in the entire world at one point, selling out massive arenas on each continent they visited. Girls routinely passed out from excitement before, during, and after the shows; there were always ambulances and medics waiting for the inevitable to occur.

"Yeah, he wants to start a solo career. He had to take some time off, which could mean anything. Hard times, disillusionment. Rehab. Whatever."

"I guess so."

I can't bring myself to think of my beloved Dustin in rehab. Not him. Not that little sweetheart. He was the youngest of the four boys in the group. The sensitive one. The cutie patootie. Even my mom used to like him.

"I have two tickets for Friday's show!" She reaches across the table and grabs my hands, and we generally squeal and freak out for a while.

Dustin. My beautiful Dustin.

Our server is laughing when she reaches the table with drinks and nachos. "Good news today, ladies?" she asks.

"You don't even know." Hayley beams. "We're going to see Dustin Grant on Friday night and my boss sort of knows him and I'm gonna introduce us."

For a second, I'm pretty sure she's going to ask us to leave. She probably thinks we've both had more than enough to drink since what just poured out of Hayley's mouth sounded like complete nonsense.

"You've gotta be kidding." The girl puts a hand to her chest, which is now heaving. Big time. "Dustin Grant? Holy shit! Oh my God, I loved him so much. I used to make out with his poster on my bedroom wall."

"My whole bedroom was practically papered with pictures of him. I honest-to-God forgot what my wallpaper looked like."

Okay, Hayley never told me that one before. And I thought I was a fan. Of course, I never got to first base with a poster like our server did either.

"And you're gonna meet him?" The girl actually squeezes my shoulder. She's right here in this moment with me. "I would give my right *anything* just to get that chance."

"Even now?" I ask, taking note of this in the back of my head.

How many women our age would still give a body part to get close to somebody like Dustin? I'm going all in on this one. I won't let my personal feelings, should there be any—there can't be; there absolutely can't be—compromise my writing. I'm sure a guy in Dustin's situation takes advantage of his position. And nostalgia.

Because dang, all of those old feelings are flooding back. I might as well be a kid again. My heart's all fluttery, and my stomach's in knots.

I will literally die if I don't marry him and have his babies.

Holy crap.

The server eventually has to go back to her job, leaving Hayley and me to freak out on our own.

"What should I wear?" I wonder. "I hate everything I own. Nothing is good enough. Do I have time to order something? No, probably not because what if it doesn't fit? I can order in every size and then send back anything that doesn't fit. Or I could go shopping at a real store, but ugh, I just did that on Saturday." I finally stop to take a breath when light-headedness sets in.

"I'm sure you have something that'll work."

"Whatever. You just wanna look cuter than me, so he'll pay attention to you."

"Ew."

"It's true!"

She holds up a hand and tosses her hair over one shoulder. "Whatever. This is all supposed to be about you, remember? For a book?"

"Please. You're telling me you'd pass up an opportunity to sleep with Dustin if he liked you better?"

Her mouth twitches. "Hey, you never know. Maybe he'll be into both of us. Maggie's been on your back about getting involved in a three-way for research, right?"

I wait to swallow a mouthful of nachos because, really, this needs to be fully understood. "Honey, I love you. And I thank you for everything you've done to help me with my career. But no."

Chapter Four

Dustin Grant.

Kitty Grant.

The wedding of Kathryn Valentine to Dustin Grant.

I can just see our wedding announcement in the Times. Talk about a meet-cute: girl writer goes to the gig of a musician whose storied career has hit the skids, but he's trying to make a comeback. They end up falling in love and getting married at The St. Regis—no, St. Patrick's Cathedral. Yes.

"I guess I should keep my name though," I mutter to my empty apartment as I kick off my shoes. *Why's it so difficult? Because we kept having martinis to celebrate my good fortune.*

Our good fortune really, but Hayley was nice enough to make it sound like this was all about me.

I can hardly think straight. This is like every adolescent dream come true.

Gosh, I wish my mom were here to fully understand this.

Just like that, my balloon pops, and I'm plopping down on the sofa. After all these years, there are still moments when it hits me like a punch to the gut. I can't call my mom to tell her I'm meeting Dustin Grant and maybe smooching him.

Heck, definitely smooching him. I'll try my damnedest to anyway.

It's been forever since I've even thought about him or the band even though they were such a huge part of my youth. Now, the memories are flooding back. I have to fire up the laptop and pull up some of their music.

Just looking at their album covers takes me back. Sitting in my room, cross-legged on the bed, staring longingly at Dustin's face. Not only his either—Kevin, Benji, and Tyler were just as cute, but they didn't have that special factor. The elusive charm.

The hours I spent listening to their music while doing homework, practicing with makeup, cuddling my teddy bear—and yes, pretending it was my favorite band member—were endless. But I didn't make out with it the way my server made out with her poster. I had standards, even at a young age.

There's already a Greatest Hits playlist made up for the band, so I hit play and sit back, ready to let the magic unfold. And oh boy, the opening chords of their first hit, "Crazy 4 You"—cleverly named after the band or maybe it was the other way around—are like a time machine. I close my eyes, and I might as well be back in Brooklyn with braces and acne and a terrible crush on the cutest boy in my Spanish class. All the girls loved him.

And when he chose to go out with the cutest girl—because honestly, who else was he going to go out with, a nerd like me?—I locked myself in my room, didn't bother turning on the lights, and listened to Dustin sing on repeat for hours on end while quietly crying. Dustin would never ignore me or look right through me, would he?

"Because … I'm crazy for you, girl …" I sing, swaying back and forth.

I still know every note. I can't remember a thing from most of my schooling back in the day, including Spanish because I was too busy crushing, but I remember every last note and word and inflection of these songs.

Maybe a little too well.

The banging from next door breaks me out of my stupor when I'm three songs in. I sit up, scowling. Leave it to Matt to burst my happy bubble.

Well, let's see how he likes this.

The next thing I know, I'm knocking at his door. Why not? I live here, too, and if he has a problem with me, he can tell me to my face. Alcohol makes me feel so brave.

It's not Matt who answers the door, which I guess shouldn't come as a surprise. There's only one reason he'd go to the trouble of knocking on his bedroom wall.

She's tall and ridiculously blonde and a little disheveled. Unless I'm mistaken, she's wearing one of his T-shirts too.

"Hi," she whispers, the door barely open a crack.

"Hi." Okay, so this isn't the most comfortable situation I've ever been in, but let's face it, it's not the most uncomfortable either. "I live across the hall and share a wall up front with Matt." I even point down the hall because, yeah, that's what people do in awkward situations.

"Oh, sure." She smiles, though the vague look on her face tells me she has no idea what to do with me.

"Anyway, sorry I was being loud; I didn't mean to. I didn't mean to be loud!" I raise my voice a little, so he can hear me, whatever he's doing. Probably plotting a way to get back at me for being obnoxious. "I mean, we've had a little thing going on for a while where I make loud noises when he's disturbing me and he does the same thing to me when I'm being too loud and you know, I've said too much. Just tell him I didn't mean it that way. I was going down memory lane, and I didn't mean to be so loud." Yeah, I'm still tipsy.

Instead of slamming the door in my face and laughing at me from the other side, she smiles. "Crazy 4 You was my favorite group ever, back in the day."

"Oh my God, me too!"

"I had the whole sheet set and pillows in the shapes of their faces."

"No way! I always wanted the pillows!"

"Yeah, my whole bed was covered with them. I probably bankrupted my parents, but what did I know?" She shrugs a little, leaning against the door. "They were my first concert too."

"I always wanted to go to their shows, but I could never score tickets."

"My dad knew a guy who was able to get them for me. I was super popular for, like, five minutes when people at school found out about it."

"Uh, Jess? Are you coming back?" Matt calls from somewhere inside the apartment.

"Yeah, be right there," she answers over her shoulder before turning to me. "Anyway, I was there for the show where that girl got onstage and tried to take Benji's clothes off and ended up getting arrested. I was close enough to see his happy trail, and I just about died on the spot."

"Lucky!"

"I know, right? I thought my fifteen-year-old heart would explode. My mom tried to cover my eyes; can you believe it?"

We both laugh over this like old friends. There are certain things in life that unite people, I guess. Juvenile puppy love is one of those things.

"Jess?" Matt's voice is a little louder this time, a little more insistent. "Still waiting for you."

"Just a second." She rolls her eyes, and I have to bite back a giggle.

"Guess what." I drop my voice to a whisper.

"I'm going to meet Dustin this weekend."

Her eyes go perfectly round. "Shut. The fuck. Up."

"I'm serious!"

"How? Where? Oh my God."

"He's doing a gig somewhere in the city. Did you not know that?" We might as well be old friends now. "Yeah, he's doing small shows on his own all over the place. You should look it up! Maybe there are still tickets. I'd have you come with us, but my friend only got two through her boss."

"Oh damn! I would love to. Do you know where it is?"

"I don't. She just told me about it tonight, which is what got me listening to the music. I'm gonna do my best to get a date with him, so I can write about it—not him specifically, but what it would be like to go out with a famous musician."

"Oh my God, you're gonna date him?" She grabs my arm. "Do you understand what I would do, even to this day, for a chance like that?"

"I'm gonna try!"

We both burst into giggles and are still giggling when Matt comes walking through the living room.

"What the hell is going on out here?" Matt eyes me with suspicion. He's shirtless and shoeless, wearing nothing but a pair of jeans he didn't bother buttoning. Speaking of happy trails, his is plainly visible.

To think, there was a time when the sight of that

would get my blood pumping. When the sight of Matt in general made me tongue-tied and awkward—even more than I usually am—because I found his hotness intimidating. Like he said, now, it feels more like we're siblings than anything else.

Which is cool. I don't have any siblings or any family at all, except my grandmother, so this works. It also means I don't have to care very much when he shoots me a dirty look for distracting his piece for the night with a trip down memory lane.

I put on my happiest smile. "We were just chatting."

"About Crazy 4 You," Jess adds.

He scratches his head, looking from one of us to the other. "You lost me."

"Big surprise." I roll my eyes at Jess, who giggles but tries to hide it.

"Sorry. I wasn't big into boy bands when I was a teenager. I didn't know that was a crime." He's still looking rather vague, which I guess is understandable under the circumstances.

"She's going to meet Dustin! The cutest one!" Jess swoons a little, which Matt does not look completely thrilled over.

I guess I wouldn't be thrilled either if a girl swooned over another guy after she came home with me.

Then, he puts it together. I can tell by the little twinkle in his eye, the twitch of his mouth.

"I thought you said it had to be a rock star."

"A musician. And he used to be one!" I can tell my defense doesn't hold water because, now, he's smirking.

"Right. Used to be. Well, I guess it's easier to hook up with a has-been than with an actual current star."

"Has-been?" Jess and I squeak in unison.

He can tell he made a mistake. "Whoops. Sorry. Didn't mean to interrupt the meeting of the fan club."

"He's not a has-been." I fold my arms, glaring at him. "And at least he has the guts to get back out there and revive his career."

"Right." Jess pokes his arm. "I'm sure there are people like you who would rather make fun of him, but at least he had a big career and was one of the most famous people in the world. Can you imagine what that would be like for a teenager? I could barely handle being a normal, regular person at that age."

"I can barely handle it now," I add.

Matt rolls his eyes. "No comment."

"That was comment enough."

Jess is still on her soapbox. "I think it's brave of him to do it."

I like this girl. It's a shame I'll never see her again. While Matt has slowed the flow of women parading in and out of his apartment, he's not one for settling down.

Would it be tacky if I asked for her phone number since we'll never see each other again otherwise? Yeah, that would probably be tacky.

"I think it's brave too."

We both stare at Matt, daring him to disagree with us.

He shrugs, giving us both the delight of seeing his bare shoulders flexing. The boy does know how to take care of himself; I'll give him that much.

"Whatever. I'm outnumbered. And now, I'm going back to my room. Not alone, I hope." He gives me one last look, containing about a million warnings to stay out of his personal business, before turning around and granting me a view of his glorious butt as he saunters back to his bedroom.

He might act like a brother to me. That doesn't mean I can't admire his body. We're not actually related.

Jess sighs like the prospect of geeking out with me is more attractive than what we just watched—and what she was probably in the middle of enjoying before my little impromptu concert began. "Anyway, I'm super jealous of you and hope you get to date Dustin. Think of it as, like, doing it for all of us. All the girls who ever dreamed he would pick them out of a crowd."

Dang it, I don't know whether to hug this girl or salute or burst into tears. "I will."

"I'd better get back to him. It was so nice meeting you!" She gives me a little wave before closing the door.

I can't wait for Matt to get on my case for interrupting him.

Chapter Five

"Noooo!"

"How do you think I feel?"

"But you have to come with me!"

"Do you think I actually want to miss this? I've only been looking forward to it all week. I bought a new dress and everything."

I can practically hear Hayley pouting on the other end of the call, where she's sitting at her desk.

I shouldn't give her a hard time about this. It's not like she wants to miss the show. But I feel really lousy now that she's told me she can't come along, thanks to work that absolutely has to be done by the end of the day. Meaning it doesn't matter whether the poor girl gets out of the office before midnight so long as it's finished.

Which means I can't just go without reminding her how much more fun it would be to have her with me. "I don't have to go tonight," I offer. "Maybe we can get tickets for another show. I can write different situations without actually needing to meet him. In fact, I don't need to meet him at all. I bet I could make something up now that I've had a little more practice in writing steamier books."

"Kitty Valentine. Are you for real?"

I don't know what to make of the stern tone she just adopted in her voice.

"I think so?"

"Do you honestly mean to tell me you would give up an opportunity like this? To fulfill a lifelong dream?"

"Let's be fair. I don't know if I would call it a lifelong dream precisely."

"You know what I mean. This is a big deal for you. I want you to go. I know it sucks, having to go by yourself, and I wish there were something I could do about it. But I absolutely won't have you missing out on this just because I have to work late on a Friday night."

"The show doesn't start until nine. Are you sure you won't have the time?"

"I'll be lucky if I leave here by then." There's so much disappointment in her voice; it just about breaks my heart. "Even if I could leave before then, I would want to freshen up, and it's not like I brought my outfit with me."

"I could go to your apartment and grab it for you, if you want. I could drop it off at your office."

"You really are too sweet." She's smiling, I can tell. But that doesn't make things any better. "Really, it's okay. Who knows? If the two of you hit it off, you could invite me to the next show. Or to your wedding."

"Hang on a second." I laugh, and my cheeks get all hot and flushed even though I know what she's saying is totally ridiculous and would never happen. "For one thing, you're the one who always reminds me that I need to keep things casual. For another thing, how the heck am I supposed to meet him if you're not there to introduce us?"

"Oh, right. Darn it, I forgot that part."

"I could still go to your apartment to get your clothes." I really wish she would give me the okay on this because I would rather not do this alone. What's the point of going to see him if I don't have her to break the ice?

"I trust you. You'll find a way to make yourself visible."

"I don't know if that's a compliment or what."

"It's definitely a compliment." She giggles. "You have a way of doing that. And if you can't think of any other way, just tell him the truth. You're there because the lawyer who works with his agent got you a ticket and encouraged you to introduce yourself. It doesn't have to be any more serious than that."

She makes it sound so easy. Sometimes, I think she forgets that not everybody is as naturally stunning and arresting as she is. That's a good word for her. *Arresting.* The sort of girl who stops conversations in their tracks just by entering a room.

Me? I've been known to stop a conversation, but

it's usually because I trip over my own feet or call somebody the wrong name or spill something on myself.

"Maybe I'll trip over a cable or break his guitar. That will catch his attention."

"That's the spirit."

I can't say I feel much better when we're off the phone. It's bad enough that I feel like a piece of garbage for going to see Dustin when we were both so excited over this, but now, I have to wonder if it's all in vain.

Regardless, I have to get myself ready—and now that Hayley won't be there with me, I have to try harder than ever to make myself interesting and appealing, so I'll catch Dustin's attention.

Which means going all out with my hair and makeup, for starters. I use a curling wand to achieve bouncy waves, and then I roll each curl around my fingers and pin them to my head, so they can cool that way while I put on my makeup. Tonight calls for something smoky, something dangerous.

It apparently also calls for three attempts at a perfect smoky eye. I've never been very good with applying the smoky-eye look. I always end up looking like a raccoon or like somebody whose makeup was flawless before they had a really difficult, drunken night. I call it the morning-after look.

Still, I think I look good by the time I'm finished, and I slide into a pair of jeans so tight that I have to do a few squats and lunges to stretch them out a bit. A loose, flowing blouse goes over them, and a pair of ankle boots completes the look along with a big necklace and chunky bracelets. Cute but not too much. I don't want him thinking I went too far out of my way for this even though it took hours and hours to finally decide on the right look.

As the clock ticks down and I come closer to the big moment of seeing Dustin in person, onstage, my heart can barely handle it. *This is it. I'm really going to meet him. Gosh, I hope my palms aren't this sweaty when the time comes.* I make a mental note to dry them on my jean jacket as I'm leaving, locking up behind me.

Perfect timing, as always, because Matt is leading Phoebe up the stairs at that very moment—or rather, Phoebe is leading Matt up the stairs.

"Hi, pretty girl!" I grin as I drop into a crouch and hope I can manage to get back up. These jeans really are tight in the legs. They're practically painted on.

Matt lets out a low whistle. "Don't you look trendy?"

"Is that supposed to be a compliment?" I eye him with suspicion.

"I don't know. I'm not sure yet." He leans against the wall, still observing me. "So, this is the big night, huh?"

"It sure is." Somehow, I manage to stand, wishing I hadn't gone quite so skinny with the jeans.

"I'm super excited."

"You know what I'm super excited about?"

Something tells me he's being sarcastic.

"Gee, I can't wait to find out."

"I'm super excited for the time when your boy-band revival comes to an end. No offense, but that's not exactly my kind of music."

"I don't remember asking whether it was your kind of music or not."

"And yet you insist upon playing it at alarmingly loud levels."

"Come on. It's not that loud."

"I have seriously considered earplugs."

"You're just being a hater."

"Be that as it may, I'm looking forward to you going back to your normal playlists."

"Careful there. I might accuse you of stalking me and pressing your ear to the bedroom wall, so you can hear what I'm listening to."

He snickers, shaking his head. "Get over yourself, Valentine. You know how thin the walls are. And for the most part, I like your taste in music. I like the old stuff better than a lot of what's referred to as music nowadays. I wasn't really into music in my teen years—not the music that was current then anyway. Honestly, I listen more to songs that were released before I was even born."

"I never knew that about you."

"I'm a man of hidden depths." He shrugs with a grin. "And when I listen to music, I keep it quiet enough that you can't hear it because I'm a thoughtful and generous neighbor." He checks his watch. "You'd better get going. Dustin won't wait all night for you to show up."

"I'm actually nervous." *Why did I just admit that? I sound so lame.*

"It's just a show. It doesn't have to be a big deal. Hayley can handle everything for you if you're nervous."

"That's the thing. Hayley can't come with me; she has to work late. Hey! Could you come?"

At least he's gentleman enough not to laugh out loud—barely. He tries to hold it in, but a few snorts slip out anyway. "Me? No, thank you. I appreciate the invitation, and let's be honest; it would probably be smart for you to have somebody there with you—to keep you from getting into trouble."

Why does he always have to add a little something at the end to be especially jerky?

"Exactly what kind of trouble do you think I could get into at a small show in a small club?"

"You don't have enough time for me to describe everything I can imagine going wrong. No offense."

"Oh, none taken."

"You'll be fine." He's not kidding anymore, he looks and sounds pretty serious, without so much as a smirk. "Go on, introduce yourself to him, and remember, he's just a regular person. That's all. Just a normal guy. You'll do fine."

That's just the trouble. It seems like I always

have problems with normal guys.

As I'm on my way down the stairs, my heart sinking in time with my descent, I have to remind myself that I am Kitty freaking Valentine, and I can have any man I want.

Can't I?

OKAY, SO THIS isn't the most impressive club I've ever been to.

Not like I was expecting much. This is a comeback tour after all. He's not going to be performing in those huge arenas anymore—and it's not like he's performing with the rest of the band either. They're all off, doing their own thing now. I think one of them just finished a season on one of those reality shows where D-list celebrities try to live in the wild or something like that.

Oh, how the mighty have fallen.

Still, it's a little dark in here. A little cramped. I descend a flight of narrow stairs, barely lit. Thank God I chose flat boots for the night. One misstep, and I would've ended up with a broken ankle. Not exactly the way I want to get Dustin's attention. I've already done the falling thing with Blake and the twisted ankle with Jake, so I'd rather pick a less embarrassing option.

A faint smell of mildew is in the air when I reach the room where Dustin is performing. There are tables all over the place in different sizes and shapes—square, round, rectangular—with mismatched chairs grouped together accordingly. The walls are papered with old promotional flyers, some of them so old that the print is barely legible. *How many performances have been given in this room? How many careers have been launched? How many have fizzled?*

I show my ticket to a man sitting near the doorway, and he points me to a table right in front, practically up against the stage. Not much of a stage, but it's a start. There are layers and layers of colored tape on the stage, I notice, where dozens and even hundreds of performers have stood on their mark.

Heck, I could write an entire short story about this club alone.

"You want something to drink?" a girl asks over my shoulder, taking me by surprise.

My imagination was too busy running away with itself for me to pay attention to anything else. I order a water. When she makes a face, I add a glass of wine. I guess people need to hustle for their tips the way I hustle to scratch out a few words and make a living.

One thing I notice as the room starts to fill up is the lack of men. For every one of them, there are at least five or six women. That doesn't exactly come as a surprise, but it is pretty funny. I bet us girls could get together and exchange stories the way I did with Jess at Matt's apartment door.

Darn it, she would've loved this. I didn't think to ask Matt if there was a way to get in touch with her. She probably would've come with me if I'd asked. I doubt he got her number, which is a shame because she seemed like a nice girl. Definitely the sort of girl I could gang up on him with.

He wants us to act like siblings? I might not have any, but I know how to play the game.

There's one table of women wearing old Crazy 4 You T-shirts, which tickles me. They're old and faded—the shirts, not the women—but they're worn with pride. The four of them giggle and whisper and look about as excited as I feel. I exchange glances with one of them and can't help but reflect on how we're complete strangers with something in common. Something that unites us. It's like a sorority in here.

The energy in the room reaches a fever pitch when the lights go down, and I can't help but feel a little giggly and fluttery. *This is it!* The event I used to dream about so desperately, what I used to wish for as hard as I could.

I hope he does a good job. It never occurred to me before this very second that he might not. What a stinking letdown it would be if he didn't.

My heart's in my throat in the moments before he steps onto the stage. When he sits on the stool and positions his guitar on his lap as the lights come up, I just about melt into my seat while my hands ache and sting from clapping as hard as I can.

Everything happens at once. I take stock of him, seeing him but also seeing the version of him I've been so used to for so long. He looks good, surprisingly good after all these years. He still has that youthful smile that shows his dimples that would drive me just about crazy. His rich dark brown hair is a little longer than it used to be, flopping over his forehead when he looks down at the guitar strings, and he pushes it back with a practiced gesture.

But it's those eyes of his. Nothing could change them. Blue like the Caribbean, so bright in the light shining on his glorious face. They're like laser beams. In the brief instant they meet mine, I can practically feel them burning into my brain.

He was cute as a kid; I know that now. I swooned over him and dreamed of what our babies would look like and was absolutely sure he was the pinnacle of human maleness. When I was barely out of puberty. But he was a kid.

Boy, is he hot as an adult. Some cute teenagers grow up to be rather unfortunate but not him. He didn't peak as a teenager. He's grown into his looks and into his body. There's a whole lot of body going on.

His tattooed arms flex when he raises his hands in acknowledgment of the applause still ringing out around the room. "Thank you," he murmurs in a deep, velvety voice.

Oh boy. Somebody fetch the extinguisher because he's setting my panties on fire.

Though really, he wouldn't have to say or do anything for that to happen. He would just have to sit there and be himself, and I would be reduced to a pile of ash.

Again, he returns his attention to his guitar as the applause quiets. "Thank you so much for coming out to be with me tonight." He sounds so humble, so shy.

My heart goes out to him. I want to wrap him in a tight hug and promise he'll never have to be alone.

What is it about him that inspires that reaction in me? That maternal, protective instinct? This is a grown man, and I'm fantasizing about rocking him to sleep in my arms. Not exactly the sort of thing I should be fantasizing about.

The second he opens his mouth and starts to sing, all other thoughts go out the window. His voice has lost the smoothness it used to have, before ten years passed and heaven knows what else. It's got a bit of a rasp to it now, like he's either a smoker or a drinker or both. But that just adds to its charm, that roughness. He used to be a little boy, but now, he's a man who's seen things, who's experienced things. He's not just singing about being crazy for a girl. That girl is gone now, and she left him facing some hard realities in her absence.

It's a beautiful song. Sweet, melodic, vulnerable. I find myself swaying along a little, wishing I knew the words so I could sing with him. Though I doubt that would be appreciated, especially in a small venue like this. When you're in an arena, you can sing your heart out, and nobody cares because everybody else is doing the same thing unless they're screaming. Same difference in the end.

By the time he strums the final chords, it's like he has me under a spell. And considering the fact that nobody around me is moving or even whispering to each other, it seems I'm not the only one. The four T-shirt–wearers are practically draped across their table, just completely gone.

If this is the way he's starting out his comeback tour, I would say he's doing a fantastic job. I'd even say he has a pretty good chance of revitalizing his career.

Though I guess my opinion isn't shared by everyone in the room.

"Play 'Break My Heart,' " somebody mutters in the back of the room, referencing probably the biggest hit Crazy 4 You ever had.

A few people hiss and boo and tell them to be quiet. I might or might not be one of them, shooting a dirty look back there. I don't know who said it, but I know the direction it came from.

Dustin is wise enough to ignore this, going into another new song. This one's a little more upbeat, about somebody who sounds a lot like him. A guy getting a second chance, who made some mistakes but wants to make good on them now. A guy with a sense of humor about himself.

Heaven help me, the kind of guy I could easily fall for. But that's just nostalgia talking—and sheer lust. I have to keep a clear head and not let my hormones dictate my evening.

"Thank you all so much for being here." He takes a look around the room once the second song is finished. "I'll be honest. I didn't think I would ever be in front of a crowd again. It's been a bumpy road, but knowing I still have fans like you out here keeps me going. I knew I had to make an effort to come back for your sake."

This earns him a warm round of applause and a few sympathetic nods. Seems like we all want to take him home and baby him. Old habits die hard.

"Play 'Break My Heart'!"

Okay, obviously somebody has had too much to drink tonight—or they're just jerks in general.

If I were Dustin, I would tell them to get the hell out. Who raised these people? Where do they get off? Yet he acts like this is all very funny, and I guess it is in a way.

"Sorry. Legally, I'm not allowed to perform those songs now." He shrugs with a hand shading his eyes from the stage lights. "That was a good time in my life though, and it's the reason you're all here now. So, I can't say anything bad about those days even if they're over. But I appreciate you wanting to revisit some old memories with me."

What a freaking gentleman. It was the perfect response—humble, gentle, measured.

But clearly not enough for the dude who's apparently obsessed with the damn song. Because of course, it's a guy because men just don't understand. Probably somebody whose girlfriend forced him into coming.

"Nobody came to hear you play your new music, dude."

That's it. I've had enough. Dustin might not be able to tell the guy off, but that doesn't mean I can't.

"Why don't you stop being such a jerk?" Before I know it, I'm standing next to my table, hands on my hips. Let the guy say something to me; I dare him at this point. "Why don't you try getting up there and singing some songs you wrote? Why don't you get up there and put your heart on display for everybody here to judge? And when you do, I'll be sure to ask you to perform something you haven't performed in at least ten years that you didn't even write and aren't allowed to sing anymore. Okay, buddy?"

By the time I'm finished, my cheeks are on fire because I realized about halfway through that I was making a massive fool of myself and should never have started on that little rant. Though I do get applause and cheers from around the room as I sit down, so I guess I wasn't completely out of line.

I would look to Dustin to see his reaction, but I can't bring myself to do it. I'm too embarrassed. I choose to focus on my wineglass instead as Dustin moves into his next song and the one after that.

It's almost a relief when the first half of his set is over, and I don't have to worry about avoiding eye contact anymore.

What was I thinking? If there's any way I could possibly make it less likely for him to want anything to do with me, I'd like to know what it is.

Maybe not because I would probably end up doing that too.

When my server comes back, I'm just about to ask for my check because, seriously, I need to get out of here. I'm so stinking embarrassed. I haven't yet figured out how I'll get by the heckler's table without causing more trouble, but maybe I can keep my head down and hurry past.

She cuts me off before I can say anything though and slides a piece of paper my way. "This is for you." She even winks before hurrying off to take care of somebody else.

For me? I slowly open it, my hands trembling.

Thanks for having my back. I'd love to thank you personally after the show. Show this to the bouncer to let you through the door to the back hall. Dustin.

Well, this is it. This is where I die because, clearly, nothing more exciting will ever happen to me in my entire life.

*T*HIS ISN'T REALLY *happening.*

It can't possibly be happening.

Clearly, I'm at home, dreaming. It's a wildly vivid dream, I'll grant you, but a dream nonetheless. Yes, I'm making this all up in my head. Because I can't truly be standing in the narrow hallway outside Dustin Grant's dressing room.

I have to remind myself to rub my hands on my jacket to get rid of the sweat because he'll inevitably want to shake my hand. Right? Isn't that how normal people usually greet each other? Oh my God, I can't believe this is happening. My teenage self would … honestly, I don't know what she'd do. Scream a lot, most likely, before passing out.

Now, I truly understand why all those girls used to pass out during Crazy 4 You concerts. And I'm not even a teenager anymore. I'm a grown woman, college-educated, four times at the top of the New York Times Best Sellers list. There is absolutely no excuse for me to fall to pieces over this man.

This man with those absolutely ridiculous eyes of his.

Focus, Valentine. *You've got this.*

But do I? I'll soon find out.

He answers almost as soon as I knock on the door. I wasn't sure he would even hear me—I'm so timid, and my knock was so quiet. Was he waiting? No, that couldn't be.

The second we're face-to-face—like, really face-to-face—I completely blank out. Seriously. It's like I have amnesia about everything in my whole entire life. Who am I? Why am I here?

And then he smiles, and things get worse. I'm almost positive I'm going to faint.

"So, you're my watchdog. I knew I had to meet you and thank you for standing up for me out there." He holds out his hand, still smiling, still showing off those dimples of his. "Dustin Grant."

"No kidding." I giggle and immediately wish I could take it back. Not exactly the ideal way to start things off. I hold out my hand to him, hoping I wiped the sweat away. "Kitty Valentine."

He blinks hard, eyes narrowing. "Really?"

"Yes, really. Why? Have you heard of me?" I can barely get it out; I'm giggling so hard.

Good God, he's going to think I'm a complete space case. This will be the last time he ever invites a fan back to his dressing room, I imagine.

So, what do I do? Easy. I keep talking because that always makes things better. "I mean, I wouldn't expect you to ever have heard of me or anything. I'm not anybody that important. Just a writer. No big deal." *Shut up, Kitty. Shut up. Stop talking. You're only making it worse.*

I'm sure Dustin has probably seen worse though. He's actually sweet, smiling a little as I continue digging myself deeper with every word.

"I find your name interesting. You say you're a writer?"

Is it possible for a human face to spontaneously burst into flames? Because I'm pretty sure that's what my face is trying to do. "Yeah, no big deal. Nothing like what you do."

He chuckles a little at this. "Or what I used to do. Like you witnessed a little while ago, a lot of my fans live in the past." He then steps back, waving an arm. "I'm so rude. Please, come in. Make yourself comfortable. I want to know all about this writing you do."

That, I cannot believe. Why would he want to know about me? I'm not that special. I've never made anybody faint just by appearing in front of them. But I step into the dressing room anyway because who wouldn't? Besides, I'm here on a mission.

Calling this a dressing room is a real stretch. Sure, it's a room, and I guess Dustin got dressed in here, but I'm thinking it normally serves as a closet. If it doesn't, it should. There's barely enough room for both of us to stand. Dustin pulls up a chair, gesturing for me to take a seat while he perches on the edge of a little shelf holding various hair products, concealer—those sorts of things.

"You know my secret now."

"Your secret?"

He gestures to the products on the table. "I wear makeup onstage."

"I'll be sure to tell all my friends."

"So, you said you're a writer?"

Darn it. I smack my forehead. "Oh, don't worry! I'm not here to write, like, an exposé on you or anything like that. I hope you didn't get that idea."

The funniest thing happens. He literally looks disappointed. At least, that's the impression I get when his face falls a little.

"Oh. I see."

"I'm a novelist. I write romance novels."

He gets another funny look, and again, I get the feeling I've said too much. Yes, this is obviously where he's going to decide I'm not worth his time. That's usually the way it happens once somebody finds out what I do and thinks it's a joke.

I'm so sure this is about to happen. In fact, I'm halfway to my feet and prepared to console myself with the fact that he has no room to talk. Who does he think he is? God's gift?

"A romance novelist." A slow smile spreads over his face, lighting it up. "That's probably the coolest thing I've heard in a long time."

Oh. That's not what I expected at all. "You think so?" I can't help but still feel a little skeptical.

"Hell yes! Seriously, that's awesome. And you

said something about me hearing about you before, right? Does that mean you're a big deal?"

Here I go again, wanting to giggle like an insane person. I'm discussing my career with none other than my adolescent fantasy. "You could say that," I offer with a shrug.

"What does that mean?" He's teasing me, trying to draw it out of me.

Is this even happening? What is my life?

"It means you could say that." *Oh my God. Am I teasing him right back? Who am I?*

The funny thing is, it feels so natural, like we're old friends already. Granted, I'm way more familiar with him than he is with me, having spent years fantasizing about what it would be like to be his wife. Back when I was so young, it never occurred to me I'd want to be anything else. Happily ever after meant a trip down the aisle, followed by a bunch of babies.

Actually, that's still what happily ever after looks like for me. But there's also happy in between and happy for now, which is definitely something I would not refuse if the man in front of me suggested it. It's one of the reasons I'm here. The chance to get to know this man, his life, his world.

Though for now, there's still hesitation on his part. I'm just a fan, and he's holding himself back from me. That's okay. This is more than enough for the time being, much more than I ever would have imagined as a kid. There's nothing worse than knowing for sure that you'll never get to be with the object of your affection because he might as well live on another planet and has no idea you're alive.

Oh, how much do I wish some of the girls from middle school were here right now? I would love to rub it in their faces.

To my horror, I realize he must've said something when I wasn't paying attention, too busy fantasizing about rubbing this in the faces of girls who haven't thought about me in years.

He's waiting with a sweet, expectant expression, those eyes of his still boring holes into me.

I have to fess up. "I'm sorry. I'm spacing out. My fifteen-year-old self is screaming in the back of my mind, and I can't seem to quiet her down."

He laughs, which is a relief. I guess he's used to it by now. "I asked if you had any plans tonight, someplace to go after this."

Hot diggity dog. I'm in. This is it. Oh my God, I'm sort of going on a date with this absolutely gorgeous, talented, charming person.

I practically have to sit on my hands to stop them from shaking. "No, I don't have any other plans."

His eyes sparkle. They literally sparkle. "Good. Because I want you to come out with me. Would you do that?" And then the dimples show up, and they're for me because he's smiling at me.

Again, I'm hit with the almost-certain feeling that I'm imagining all this and that it can't possibly be happening. But that doesn't stop me from answering, "Yes?"

For the first time since I came into the room, it looks like I've knocked him off his game a little. "Is that a question? Or are you agreeing?"

"I'm agreeing!" Great, and now, I sound like I'm screaming. I really wish I could go back and start this all over again, but I can't. "Yes. I would very much like to come out with you." I manage to sound like a mature, sane person this time.

"Great." He stands up, and I do the same. "Just give me a minute, would you?"

I nod. He can have all the time he needs.

He lifts his brows. "I mean, could I have a minute to get myself ready? Alone?"

Yep. I knew I would do something else to embarrass myself. "I'm sorry. I swear, I'm usually much better at acting like a normal person than this." That's pretty much a lie, of course, but he doesn't need to know.

He chuckles softly, rubbing a hand over the back of his neck with his eyes downcast. "No worries. Not to sound too full of myself, but I get it a lot. I mean, I can't understand why anybody would care all that much about me, but you're not the first person, so it's okay. You don't have to feel weird."

He has no idea what a good job he's doing of convincing me that I wasn't wrong for being so madly in love with him all those years. My instincts are good, even back then. I know quality when I see it.

I duck out of the room before I have the chance to say anything that could embarrass me any more and use the opportunity to text Hayley. It feels kind of mean, reaching out to her about this when she can't be here, but I have to tell somebody, and something tells me she would never forgive me if I didn't give her the play-by-play.

Oh my God. We're going out now. I don't know where, but does it matter? He's a dream. Even better-looking in person.

She must've been waiting to hear from me because barely five seconds pass before she's typing a reply. *Oh my God, I hate you so much. See if you can grab something of his for me.*

I have to work hard to keep from laughing out loud, especially because I know it would come out as one of those high-pitched laughs, totally unhinged. I'm sure he'd be able to hear me in the dressing room, and I've already embarrassed myself enough.

What did you have in mind? I ask her.

I don't care! A napkin, whatever. Anything that has his DNA on it.

Okay, now, she's starting to make me nervous.

What do you plan on doing? Making a clone?

No, I just want a little piece of him for myself. Don't make it weird.

I'm the one making it weird?

I'll see what I can do, I reply since that's the best I can say. It would be one thing if I even thought she was joking, but I get the feeling that she's not.

Who am I kidding? I would probably do the same thing if our places were reversed.

It's not long before the door opens, and Dustin beams his beautiful smile on me. "Ready?"

I'm not entirely sure I am ready, but there's nothing to do but say, "Yes."

Chapter Eight

OKAY, THIS ISN'T exactly what I had in mind, but it's strangely fitting, considering the way the night started out.

Dustin takes a deep breath when we step into the little dive bar he's brought me to. "This is it," he murmurs, looking over the room.

I'm lost already. "This is what?" *Do I sound cool enough?* I hope I do. I probably don't.

He smiles anyway. "The real deal. This is life. Not some prefabricated band, not some orchestrated version of life created for cameras and reality television. This is it. This is what I missed for a long time."

I get what he means, though I do sort of wish we could've gone someplace where my shoes don't stick to the floor if I stand in one place for too long. It's dark in here, cramped, and even though smoking in public places has been against the law for years, there's still a lingering odor of it. It clings to every surface, and I guess it could be called atmospheric.

But come on. I'm out with Dustin, which is a

freaking dream come true. It doesn't matter where we are or if it smells like decades of old smoke in here.

"So, you feel more comfortable here than you do in that other world you just described?"

It's not until we sit at a corner table, a high top, secluded from a lot of the room, that he answers my question, "So much more comfortable. I'm a real person here. I missed that for a long time. You have no idea how it messes with a person's head, being told they're the best when they're barely out of puberty."

I could eat every word with a spoon. This is the kind of stuff I want to know, not just for a book I've barely scratched the surface of writing yet, but for the fact that I want to know him. This is the sort of real-life, intimate information I would've killed for back in the day. Even hearing it now gives me a little thrill—which is weird because he's talking about something that once made him very unhappy. Maybe I shouldn't be so thrilled, come to think of it.

"That must've been really hard for you."

He turns his head as if giving me a skeptical look I can feel, even with the presence of those dark sunglasses he insists on wearing. I mean, let's be reasonable. Anybody who sees somebody walking around in sunglasses in the middle of the night, in a dive bar that's already dark enough, is going to know straight up that he's a celebrity. Part of me wonders if it's a little performative, designed to attract attention instead of repelling it.

Then again, what do I know? I don't know his life. I don't know what he's been through. But I most definitely have heard him being heckled for no longer fitting into the little box a record company once put him in years ago.

He must decide I'm for real because all he does is sigh deeply while nodding his head. "On the outside, things were incredible. Amazing, a dream come true. The money I earned back then bought my family a new house. It put my younger sister through school, and I was happy to do it. It would've put me through school, too, if I hadn't thought I was hot shit and decided not to go past high school. And even then, it was just tutoring. There was no way I could have gone to a regular school back then."

"You would've been torn to pieces on the first day."

He snickers, lifting a hand to signal the nearest server. "Something like that. But the real problem, according to the principal and all the faculty at my local high school, was the distraction I would pose to the other kids. In other words, it was their education that would get screwed up if I were around. And don't get me wrong; I totally get it. I'm sure they had a point. But at the time, it felt like a slap in the face."

"I can totally understand that."

Of course, I can also understand their point of view too. Who was more important? One student or every other student who would inevitably forget all about schoolwork in favor of the superstar in their school?

A server who looks to be around my age approaches. There's a question in her eyes when she looks from Dustin to me, and I'm about ready to burst with the knowledge that, *Yes, your assumption is correct.* It's really him. He orders a whiskey, neat, and I decide it's better to stick with wine since that's where I started out. I'm having a drink with him. I'm actually having a drink with him! The server takes her time turning around, and by the time she goes to the bar and mutters something to the bartender, I get the feeling she's onto us—or rather, onto him since I might as well be halfway across town for all she cares.

There's a pretty decent band playing, and Dustin is getting into the music, his head bobbing up and down. "This is the kind of thing I want to be able to do," he confesses as he nods toward the stage at the far end of the bar.

"Really? I mean, that's great," I'm quick to add when he looks at me. "But is that satisfying for you after everything you've already done? I know it sounds hopelessly naive."

That earns me a smile. "A little naive. Not hopelessly, but a little. And yeah, I really mean it. I've had the fame and fortune. I don't want that anymore. I just want to play my music and be respected as an artist, not seen as a has-been or a failure—or worse yet, a warning to other musicians. That's the worst—when you're held up as some sort of example of what not to do if you ever make it big."

I'm about to ask him what that means, what he did exactly—*is that rude? Maybe*—when we're joined by our server and one of her friends.

"I'm so sorry," the girl whispers, leaning in much closer than she needs to, "but are you Dustin Grant? Because you look just like him."

When he smiles, a little sheepish, the other girl points. "The dimples! I told you. As soon as I saw the dimples, I knew it was him!"

He admits that, yes, he is the one and only Dustin Grant and even submits to having selfies taken with both of them. Naturally, I'm not included in any of this. One of them even bumps into me as she's scrambling around, trying to get as close to him as possible. She doesn't even acknowledge coming into contact with me, too busy flipping out over him.

At least he looks genuinely pleased to be recognized. He's not a jerk about it the way I've heard some celebrities can be. I've seen it before with my own eyes too—you don't live in Manhattan without bumping into the occasional famous person. I mostly try to play it cool because I'm afraid somebody will get angry with me for invading their personal space while they're only trying to pick up a loaf of bread or something quick for dinner.

Clearly, neither of these girls cares very much about Dustin's personal space, putting their arms around him and generally draping over on him like clothes on a hanger. It's hard not to laugh a little, but I stop myself by remembering how I giggled so hard that I almost passed out when we met less than an hour ago. I have yet to earn the right to be smug over being the girl sitting next to him.

But that doesn't mean I'm not a little smug, just the same.

"Do you get that a lot?"

We're alone again—or as alone as we're going to be for the rest of the night. Now that word is starting to spread, things are getting interesting. People are craning their necks to get a better view, whispering to each other, nudging each other. Probably daring each other to approach him. He seems to be taking it all in stride, accepting his drink with a murmured thanks.

"Something tells me I'm about to get a lot more of it. I'd be the worst liar if I told you this was a huge inconvenience. It can be, for sure, but this is nothing. Your hair would go white if I told you just half of what I've put up with over the years. Girls sneaking into my room, disguising themselves as hotel employees, trying to crawl through ventilation ducts—"

"No kidding!" I should totally be writing this down.

He nods slowly. "That's nowhere near the worst of what I saw. Honestly, for as young as they were, those girls were pretty creative. It finally got to the point where I would have to send a bodyguard into my hotel room to sweep it for anybody hiding in the closet or under the bed before I even stepped in."

"That's wild."

"That's fame." He's already through with his drink and signaling for another.

By now, the girls are practically clawing each other's eyes out for the opportunity to be the one to bring him a refill.

I can't help it. I'm feeling a little full of myself right now. I mean, who wouldn't? I'm the lucky girl sitting next to him. The one having a conversation with him—not because I brought him a drink, but because he asked me out. Me! He asked me out! Just thinking it is enough to make me want to start giggling all over again.

"What about you? You haven't said much about yourself."

He's not wrong about that, but it's because we've been talking about him since we arrived. Not that I mind. Even if I wasn't writing a book about a rock star, I would want to hear all about him. I could drink him in with a straw and never get tired of it.

"Me? My life is extremely dull compared to yours."

"That's all in the past though. That's not the present."

"Those three women over at the next table who are trying to convince themselves to come over here is happening very much in the present moment." I nod my head in their direction, where the three of them are giggling furiously behind their hands, trying to get a picture of him in the extremely low light.

"You are what I want to know about though." He actually goes so far as to remove his glasses, and he leans in until we're practically nose to nose.

Did I die? Is this heaven?

My laughter is a little breathless, a little giddy. "I'm afraid I'll disappoint you."

"I doubt you could ever disappoint anybody if you tried."

"I'm afraid if you made a bet on that, you would lose."

"I like my chances." And then he touches my leg, and my soul leaves my body for a second. "What do you say we get out of here? There's a little too much attention now that you mention it, and I wanna get to know you better."

Oh. This is happening so fast. Why doesn't my mouth want to work? I moisten my lips with my tongue since my mouth is now as dry as a desert. *What do I say? What's the right thing to say in a situation like this?*

In other words, what is the non-Kitty thing to

say?

He laughs softly, probably picking up on my immediate discomfort. "I'm starving. Doesn't look like they have any food here, and I haven't eaten since lunch. Eating right before a performance is never a good idea. It's bad enough that I'm trying to get back out there, but nobody wants to hear me burp in the middle of a song."

I can't help but think back to Blake and how I ruined what could have been a beautiful evening with a rather bassy belch of my own. I don't think there will ever be a time when I don't cringe at the memory.

"Yeah, let's get something to eat. Whatever you want."

Anything so long as it means spending more time with him. It feels like this is such a magical night, the sort of experience that only comes once in a lifetime. I want it to last as long as possible.

Chapter Nine

"BEST PIZZA IN the city." Dustin hands me a slice with extra cheese, so big that it needs two paper plates to hold it.

"It's bigger than my head!"

"Good thing it's so amazing then." He flashes a killer smile before folding his slice in half and taking a huge bite. His eyes close, and he groans in a way that just about curls my toes.

What would it take for a girl to make him sound like that without the pizza?

One bite, and I realize I could never make him sound that way because, good Lord, this is some incredible pizza. The thing about living in New York is, every pizza joint claims it's the best, just like every bagel shop and every sandwich shop claims they're the greatest thing that ever happened to their individual type of food.

But this stuff is no lie.

"Oh my goodness. I wish I'd worn stretchy pants."

"I'm glad you didn't. Those are really working for you."

Sweet Jesus, he's checking me out and not being subtle about it. His eyes crawl over me. I don't bother reminding him that my eyes are further north.

"They won't be working if I eat much more of this." I take another bite for lack of any other way to respond to his attention. I mean, sure, it's amazing and incredible and a dream come true, but it's more than a little overwhelming too. Like getting the moon and not knowing what to do with it. I don't want to tell him to stop, but I'm at a loss for how to handle him.

"Come on then." He holds the door open for me. "Let's get out of here and walk some of this off as we eat."

"You know we'll have to walk to Staten Island and back to even begin to burn it off, right?"

Of course, I follow him because, all things considered, I'm having a really good time. Even better than I would've imagined. Underneath the whole fame thing, he's just a person. A real person who really just wants to be able to get a piece of pizza and live a normal life. I don't know why that means so much to me, but it does. It makes me like him so much more than if he were just some egomaniac out for a quick good time with a fan.

Let's be honest. There's nothing wrong with that either, if both parties are into it.

But I'm a big girl. I can take care of myself. And even though my loins practically burst into flames every time he looks at me, I think I'm handling things pretty well.

"You probably think I'm the biggest dick in the whole world," he informs me as we walk.

One thing I love about New York is how there's always something happening, always something going on, no matter what time it is. It's now well after two in the morning, but there are still people wandering around, laughing, eating huge slices of pizza like we are.

I shoot him a look. "Why would I think that?"

"Because I keep telling you I want to know about you, but we end up getting back on the subject of me. I promise, I'm not usually this self-centered."

"I don't think you're being self-centered. And honestly, I'm not trying to be cute when I tell you there's not that much to know about me. There really isn't."

"You said you're a romance writer, right?"

"That's right."

"Do you self-publish? Or do you do the traditional publishing thing?"

Just the fact that he even thinks to ask that question is impressive. I can't help but smile. "Traditional publishing."

"Impressive. Good sales?"

"I hope you won't think I'm bragging."

He laughs. "That answers my question."

"I'm really not trying to brag!"

"Why not? You might as well. You're successful. Own it. You deserve it. So, really"—there's a teasing note in his voice, and it matches well with the teasing look in his eye—"what are we talking about here? Any best sellers?"

I can't help but blush as I hold up four fingers.

His laughter echoes against the tall buildings around us. "Shut up! Are you serious? Four best sellers?"

"Well, four number ones, and the rest have hit somewhere on the list. I've been very lucky."

"That's not luck. That's talent. You must be a hell of a writer. The only people I know who made it to the *New York Times* list are people whose memoirs were written by ghostwriters. Not the same thing. That's so neat."

The fact that he uses the word *neat* is probably the most endearing thing about him so far. I can't help it.

"It is pretty neat," I have to admit. "And now, here I am. Having pizza with you. I don't think I could ever come up with a scenario from one of my books that would top this."

"Well, that's a nice compliment."

"I mean it. I'm not just saying that. This is … this is a real thrill. I know that sounds corny. But it's true. I would never have guessed something like this could ever happen. Would you forgive me if I told you I kind of feel like Cinderella right now?"

"Oh, no way." But he's smiling when he says it.

"But I'm not that big of a deal. I learned a long time ago not to listen to my own press."

I'm watching him with my writer's mind clicking away in the background. Not just as a fan either and not just as a woman in the grip of a dizzying, heart-stopping crush—even if that's exactly who I am and exactly what I'm dealing with.

It makes it difficult for me to be in the moment sometimes, even if the moment is one I very much want to be in. Like right now. I wish I could soak in the glory of being with him and leave it there, but I can't stop thinking. Watching him. Noticing the way he reacts when people recognize him. People who, like me, probably haven't thought about him in a very long time. The sight of him brings back so much nostalgia.

In a way, I feel sorry for him because those people don't care about him right now. They only care about who he used to be to them.

Strangely enough, he's thinking along the same lines. "It's funny how many people stop caring about you when you're not on top anymore," he murmurs.

"I can't imagine."

"No, you can't. Consider yourself lucky. You're on top."

I could tell him a thing or two about that, but I choose not to. It might end up sounding ridiculous compared to what he's been through.

"You saw how it was tonight. With everybody

expecting me to be who they wanted me to be. Because that's all they think I am. Just the guy who used to sing with that band years ago. God forbid I have my own music, something I want to say. All they want is what they remember. Not who I am now."

Yes, I can most definitely relate on a smaller scale. "I know what it means to feel boxed in by people's expectations," I say in a quiet voice.

"Yeah, I'm sure." Okay, so maybe that wasn't the best thing for me to say because, now, he sounds irritated.

My face must reflect how bad I feel about that because he immediately softens.

"I'm sorry. I'm being moody and morose, like my manager calls it. His exact words. Only he deserves it most of the time, but you don't. Please, don't take it personally. I'm acting like a dick, but that has nothing to do with you since you've been nothing but sweet."

"I'm sure you're very frustrated," I offer. "Just know that one pigeonholed artist understands what another artist is going through."

He comes to a stop, which means I do too. I feel his eyes moving over me, studying me. It's not unpleasant even if I've never been very good at handling attention. But this isn't the same as suffering through Hayley going overboard with compliments.

"You called me an artist." It comes out almost in

a whisper, like he's afraid to say it too loud. Like he's scared I'll say he misheard me and laugh about it.

He didn't, and I wouldn't.

"I did. That's what you are. Sure, back in the day, you were part of … well, sort of part of the machine. You did what you were told to do, sang the music you were told to sing, all that. But now, you want to get back out there and make something real for yourself. Right? Isn't that true?"

"Absolutely." He's gazing at me with so much intensity; I can barely breathe. He takes one step closer to me and then another. "That's exactly what I want. How did you know? How did you see so easily?"

"I don't know," I confess with a soft giggle. It's impossible not to feel a giddy surge of excitement when he looks at me the way he is right now. "I see you, I guess. I understand at least a little. And I saw you up there on that stage tonight; you were so brave."

He snickers softly, shrugging. "Brave? I don't know about that." A little smile plays over his face just the same, so I can tell he likes that I said it.

The sensation of his hand touching mine is roughly what I'd imagine an electric shock feeling like. It's a spark that runs up my hand, my arm, and then all through me. It lights up my brain and my heart and my insides.

But he holds himself back from more than that,

and I don't notice that he's nervous until his gaze darts away from mine and over my shoulder.

"I want to kiss you," he admits, though he's still not looking at me.

Okay. Not the most romantic way of telling me. "Thank you?"

He doesn't see the humor. "I'm still a little paranoid about doing things like that out in public. I know it's dumb. But I've had my life blasted all over the world for so long ..."

"I get it." And I do. I'd be paranoid too. "I remember some of the things they used to say. I don't know how you put up with it."

"I didn't do such a good job—but I don't want to talk about that right now."

Instead, he pulls me along with him to the curb and hails a cab. We take the first one that comes up, and I follow him inside without asking why we're doing this or where we're going.

Certain situations, you don't stop to question. Like looking a gift horse in the mouth. Not a good idea.

"Drive around." Those are the only two words Dustin mutters to the driver before practically pulling me into his lap.

Our mouths are so close.

This is happening. I can feel it. I can smell his cologne and the pizza and whiskey on his breath, and I can hear blood rushing in my ears as he takes my face between his hands and brushes his lips against mine. It's sweet, tentative, gentle.

And hot. Hot as hell, hot enough to make my nerves tingle and my lady bits sing the "Hallelujah" chorus.

And that's before he plunges his tongue between my lips, and I just about explode. Somebody taught him how to kiss, and he took detailed notes. His hands leave my face in favor of running through my hair while my hands slide over his chest and shoulders.

This is real. It's real!

His heart's pounding in his chest, under my palm. He's feeling this too.

When he takes me by the hips and pulls me closer, I can tell other parts of him are also responding. If I wasn't in the middle of the hottest make-out session of my life, I'd have to pinch myself.

Dustin Grant, with his tongue in my mouth and his erection pressed up against me, groans softly as his hands run up and down my back. Not moonlight and roses, but it's pretty darn good in the moment.

"Let's go to my hotel," he whispers in my ear before nibbling on my neck.

I can barely hold a single thought in my head, but that invitation rings out like a gong and sweeps everything else away for a second. "Your hotel?"

"Yes." He thrusts his hips against me. "I need you. Now."

Sure. Why not?

That goes through my head right away because I'm only human, right? This onetime music god wants to take me back to his hotel and rock my world. And it's all in service of my book after all. Isn't it?

Somewhere deep in the back of my mind, I know what this will lead to. It might be a great night, one for the books—no pun intended—but that'll be it. I'll be one more girl to add to his list of conquests, and I don't want to be that girl.

So, even though every part of my body wants desperately to give in and go to his hotel and let him ravish me, I pull back and look him in the half-lidded eye. "I can't do that. I want to, but I can't."

His eyes snap open wide. "What?"

"I said, I can't do that. I want to. But that's not how I am."

He snorts softly like this is news to him. "You're serious?"

"I am." I wiggle out of his lap even though my heart's sinking and my lady parts are not happy with me right now. I'm afraid they'll stage a revolt.

He stares at me, frowning, straightening himself out. "Wow. Okay. I've gotta say, that's new."

"I guess it is." But I won't apologize even though I'm sure I ruined my chances for this to go anywhere else. *Man, I always make the wrong move! It wouldn't have hurt anything for me to say yes, would it?* I'd have had an incredible memory and a heck of a story to share with Hayley.

And Matt because he needs to have it rubbed in his face. Why he should come to mind right now is a mystery.

"Where do you wanna go?" He's still looking at me like I'm some unknown species.

Is it really that unusual for somebody to turn him down? I mean, the law of averages says he's had to have been turned down at some point, right? The girls he picks up can't all be willing.

Jeez, how could I have been so dumb? This whole night was nothing more than a drawn-out pick-up for him. He took me for drinks, for pizza, for intimate conversation while walking the streets of New York. A magical, dizzying sort of experience he hoped would knock me off my feet and into his bed.

No wonder people think I'm naive.

"I think I should go home." I wrap my arms around myself and look out the window, away from him. "I really want to go with you, Dustin. I really do. But I can't. Not when I don't know you."

It's a long time before he says anything. When he does, it sounds like he's trying not to laugh. "You're different. I'll give you that. I can't remember the last time somebody turned me down. Is it me? Did I do something wrong?"

"No! No, you're … you! You're amazing. But I'm not going to sleep with you just because you are who you are. What's the point?"

He snickers.

"I mean, okay, I get what the point is," I admit. "But I'm the kind of girl who wants to know somebody when she's with him like that. I know I'm old-fashioned. But I can't be somebody I'm not."

He hates me. I can feel it. I can hardly even blame him because I sort of hate myself. No, I won't go back on my principles, not even for him. But dang it, this is unfortunate.

I give the driver my address and tell myself he's not laughing at this situation, though I'm sure he heard everything that just happened and finds it humorous. How many situations like this has he witnessed? I wonder if I'm the only girl who's ever turned down a famous musician.

We travel most of the way in silence with Dustin's knee jogging up and down like he's nervous or annoyed. It's not until we reach my block that he asks, "Can I at least have your number? I'd love to see you again."

Yeah, right. This is his version of letting me down easy, I bet. He doesn't want me thinking he was only out for one thing. I might spread the word and give him a bad reputation while he's in the middle of his big comeback.

"Sure. I'd love it if you did."

And I would. I hope he calls.

I just doubt he will.

Chapter Ten

"WELP, THERE GOES that." I offer a shrug as I sit back in my chair with a latte in hand.

It was a late night, and I'm not used to being out late. Working late, sure. But being out and social and whatnot is something completely different.

In other words, I need caffeine. A sympathetic ear is nice, too, which is where my best friend comes in.

Hayley sighs, putting her chin in her hands. "Wow. What a night. Would you ever have guessed you'd do something like that? Turn down Dustin Grant?"

Okay, she could've chosen better words, but … "Have you completely forgotten who you're talking to?"

We share a laugh over that, though my heart's not in it. I still can't believe I passed up an opportunity I'll never have again.

"I bet he was pretty pissed," she sighs, swirling the celery stalk in her Bloody Mary before taking a sip.

"Oh well. He can deal with it. Did you forget

you're my best friend and you're supposed to be comforting me right now?"

"Of course I haven't forgotten that, you dork." She scowls, shaking her head. "I'm just saying, I almost wish I could've been there to see how he reacted. That's my point. He probably didn't know what to do."

"He did seem sorta shocked."

"I'm sure. Can you imagine how many girls he's probably banged? Hundreds."

"Ew."

"But it's probably true. Who knows how many STDs you avoided by turning him down?"

"Not while I'm eating." As it is, my veggie omelet doesn't look as appetizing as it looked before she reminded me of all the diseases Dustin might be carrying.

"I'm trying to help you feel better."

"I think you're feeling a little smug at how everything turned out."

"Noooo." But her eyes are twinkling.

"Hayley."

"All right, all right." She gets serious, arms folded on the table, leaning in. "You did the right thing. It's not like you to fall into bed with just anybody even if it's the gorgeous, amazing, love-of-your-life."

"Wow. You're making me feel so much better now. Thank you, best friend." I'm starting to wish I'd ordered a boozy drink to help me manage the conflicting feelings I'm battling this morning.

"I can't help it. Part of my job as your best friend is to rub your cute little nose in situations like this, where you passed up on a once-in-a-lifetime opportunity."

"Oh my God. I'm gonna kill you."

"Okay, okay. I'm finished. I swear." But her lips are twitching as she goes back to her waffle.

"You think I should've gone with him?"

"No. I absolutely don't." She glances up at me. "One hundred percent no. You did the right thing for you. Not everybody would've stuck to their guns in that situation, but you did. And I expect nothing less from you by now."

"Well, thanks for that."

"You still sound bummed," she points out before popping a piece of waffle into her waiting mouth.

"I am! Because that's it. He'll never call; he'll never text. I'm sure he deleted my number the second I was out of the cab."

"Do you honestly think he was lying to you about being a nice person? About liking you?"

"You don't think so?"

"I love you, so of course I don't think he was lying. I think you charmed him, the way you charm just about everybody."

That makes me laugh. "Please. You're just saying that."

"If that's what you wanna think." She shrugs,

throwing her hair over one shoulder. "But it's true. I think he found you refreshing."

"You weren't even there."

"You didn't hang all over him, did you?"

"No."

"You didn't try to use him somehow, like scoring an expensive night out?"

"Of course not."

"I'm sure he's not used to that, and he probably really liked it. You treated him like a real person."

"I did keep telling him how special it was to be with him though."

"Probably just enough to make him feel like a big deal. From what you're telling me, you did everything just right. He felt flattered and important but not so important that you became just another girl. Just one of many who are always trying to lock him down. You stood out." She's wearing her killer smile by the time she's finished, the one I'm sure will win over every jury she'll ever be in front of.

Though it's not convincing me right now. "You weren't there. You didn't see or hear how disappointed he was."

"Forget him then." She shrugs before picking up her drink. "He's not worthy of you."

"You're serious? You've been drooling over him all week, flipping out that we were going to meet him, and now, he's not worthy of me?"

"Anybody who'd brush you off because you

didn't want to sleep with them right after you met isn't worthy of you. End of story." She takes a sip of the drink before shrugging again. "I mean, I would have slept with him, but that's just me."

"What?" It comes out a little too loud, as usual. There will come a day when people start asking me to find somewhere else to eat and drink. I'm sure of it.

"What?" she counters, arms folded. "That's just me. I would've done it. But you're not that girl."

"I can't believe you."

"What did I say?"

I have to laugh even though there's nothing funny going on right now. "You just got done telling me I avoided a walking, talking STD, and now, you're saying you would've slept with him?"

"I would've insisted on condoms, obviously."

"So would I! What, do you think I'm that naive?"

"I was trying to make you feel better!"

"It didn't work!"

"I know that now!"

We both sit there, breathing a little heavy, faces flushed.

"What are we even yelling about?" I finally ask.

"I don't remember." She starts laughing, which gets me going too. "I'm sorry. I wasn't trying to make you feel bad, I swear. If I were you, I would've gone through with it, if only because there's no way I'd ever find myself in that situation again. You know me. I don't like to let opportunities pass me by."

"But I do?"

She's making me feel worse by the second. I'm wondering why I even came out to brunch with her. This was supposed to be a sympathy brunch, a boost-my-confidence brunch. But here I am, a loser who likes letting opportunities pass her by.

"You don't see things the way I do. There's nothing wrong with that. You stayed true to yourself. That's what matters most."

Is she right? I guess so. I know I see it that way, but that doesn't make me right.

"I guess it doesn't matter anyway. I got plenty of ideas from him last night. I know the direction I want this to go in. I can always fill in the blanks with things I make up. It's all good."

It doesn't feel so good. It feels awful. Because now that it's the morning after and I'm thinking back, I wish I weren't so stinking principled. I missed out on the chance to say I'd once slept with Dustin Grant.

Though, really, is that such a prize? Maybe back when I was a teenager, and since he's a few years older than me, it would've been pretty illegal for us to hook up then. By the time I reached eighteen, Crazy 4 You wasn't a presence in my life anymore. Or in anyone's probably. Except for the boys in the group.

Now? "He's just a person who used to be famous. Now that I think about him that way, it's sort of sad. But it's the truth. Nobody wants him for who he is now. Only who he used to be."

"Oh, that's good." Hayley nods, wide-eyed. "I love that. You need to make sure that's a big part of your book."

"Thank you so much for your help."

"Don't be mad at me."

"I'm not mad." I'm a little mad.

"Right. And we just met and I don't know anything about you and I can't read every twitch of every muscle in your face."

"I just have to get over it, is all. I'm mad at myself, honestly. Not at you. Who knows? He might not have brushed me off after we slept together. I might've pulled out my expert sex moves and won him over. I mean, that's the sort of crap I write about, isn't it? I'm sure it must happen for somebody, somewhere."

"I love that you call it crap."

"But I'm right, aren't I? I could've stolen his heart through my ninja-level sex skills."

"Since when do you have those?" She lifts a skeptical eyebrow.

"Um, since I started watching a lot of porn to inspire my writing. Obviously. I've learned a thing or two. Granted, I haven't had a chance to use any of those skills, but that only means I'll seriously blow the mind of the next guy I sleep with."

Which, of course, is when our cute, young male

server, who's been trying to catch Hayley's eye throughout our entire meal, just happens to clear his throat—right by my side. "I was going to ask how everything's going here." He sounds both confused and intrigued, and he's not looking at Hayley anymore.

"Great," I croak, staring across the table in hopes that Hayley will help me out of this.

Which, of course, she does not. "Interested?" she asks, gesturing to me. "She's been studying and everything."

"Just kidding!" I laugh while kicking her under the table.

Since I'd rather gouge my eyes out with a knife than look at him right now, I keep my eyes glued on Hayley until he goes away.

"He looked interested," Hayley says with a smirk.

"I hate you so much. Do you and Matt get together and come up with ways to mess with me? Because that's something he would've done." I plunk my head down on my arms that are crossed over the table.

"I knew I liked him." When I don't smile, she sighs. "Would you relax? I'm trying to shake you out of this funk you put yourself in. Stop being so serious and dramatic and take your head off the table."

"No," I mumble.

"Kitty, you just said you have all you need for

your book, which was the entire purpose of this little exercise. And now, you can say you made out with Dustin. In the back of a cab. Kitty, that's hot."

I raise my head a little. "It was pretty hot."

"And I am extremely jealous."

That lifts me a little more. "I mean, it's not that I'm glad you're jealous … but I'm not, not glad."

Chapter Eleven

"HOW OLD WERE *you when everything started?"*

He looked up at the starless night sky, frowning a little like he had to think about it. When was the last time anybody had asked him that question? Did anybody care anymore? From what she'd seen earlier in the evening, she guessed the answer was no—and it made her so sad to think about it. He had so much more to offer than just a few songs and a killer smile.

"I had just turned fourteen. They liked me because I was cute and because my voice hadn't changed yet. I could still hit the falsetto notes they wanted."

She waited for more, but nothing came. "That's it?" she asked after a while.

"What did you expect?"

She shrugged, searching for a way to put words to her feelings. "I don't know. I guess it sounds stupid and naive, but I figured maybe the producers saw something special about you that told them you were the right person. A little spark or a light in your eyes or your smile. Or in the way you sang."

He came to a stop, standing in front of her. Right now, in the middle of the night, in the middle of the park, he was just another guy. There was no artifice, no fans jockeying to get closer to him so they could take his picture. He wasn't putting on that signature, I know I'm in public so I'd better look pleasant expression she had already seen so many times in the few short hours they'd spent together.

He was just a guy, and he was looking at her. She told herself to ignore the thrill that ran up her spine, right along with the wish that her best friends from middle school were there to see this. They'd never believe it.

He looked so serious, almost stern. The fact that he reminded her of her father went a long way toward tamping down the impulse to throw herself into his arms. "Do you want to know the truth? Do you think you can handle it? Having your expectations blown to bits, I mean."

She nodded, silent, holding her breath in anticipation. He was going to tell her some great secret, she could just tell. How many years had she wanted him to look at her this way? How many times had she imagined him trusting her with his private, personal information? How many times had she wished for him to think of her as something rare?

He drew in a deep breath and slowly let it out. "I was young, I was cute, I could carry a tune. They already had two blonds in the group and wanted another dark-haired kid to balance things out. It came down to me and another blond, and I got the job because of my hair."

She swayed a little, blinking hard, processing this. "And?"

"And what?"

"Is there more to the story than that?"

His smile was sad, cynical. "No, there isn't, which is exactly why I'm telling it to you. That was the entire reason I got chosen for the group. I had brown hair, and the other kid they liked had blond hair. I wonder what he's doing with his life now."

Why did it hit her like a punch in the gut? She was an adult now, not a little kid anymore, and she had seen enough of the music industry in the few short years she'd spent working in it to know things like what he'd described happened all the time.

Sure, on the outside, there was a lot of mystique and glamour.

People wanted to believe what they wanted to believe about their favorite artists. Maybe it was a deep-seated hope that truly hard work and talent would win the day. Maybe they were dreaming of a future for themselves in the industry and thought they could make it big if they wanted it badly enough.

Yet here in front of her stood proof that, sometimes, all that mattered was the color of a person's hair and whether or not their voice had changed by the age of fourteen.

"You look upset." He took a step closer, frowning, his eyes appearing darker. Maybe it was the concern in them, or maybe it was the fact that she wasn't used to looking at him without a spotlight in his face.

"Not upset," she insisted with a faint smile, "but sad."

YES. THAT'S HOW I felt when Dustin and I were talking. Granted, I don't know if any of what I just said reflects his experience, but it feels true to me. Besides, it's true to my characters, and that's what really matters.

My heroine is a publicist assigned to rehab the image of a former boy-band member who wants to make it on his own. She was a huge fan of his back in the day, and meeting him as an adult is a real bucket of ice water over her head. He's nothing like she expected, nothing like she used to imagine when she was a kid. Back then, when she adored him, he was heavy into drugs and alcohol. Now, he's moody, insecure, and it irks him to no end when people insist on thinking of him as the teenage superstar he used to be.

Not so far from reality, it seems, though my hero is much more temperamental and self-obsessed than Dustin struck me.

Of course, he has a heart of gold underneath all those insecurities, and of course, my heroine is the key that unlocks the door he hid his heart behind to protect himself at a young age. He got hurt one too many times and decided to never get hurt again. Once he realizes she's the real deal, not like the users he used to know, he opens up, and they create something real together.

Or so I tell myself. I'm still in the early stages of building these characters and the way they fit together, but I'm liking the direction this is headed in. Maggie likes it too—or at least, she pretended to.

No, on second thought, my editor never pretends to like something she doesn't like.

"So long as they bone frequently," she reminded me before we got off the phone earlier today.

Yes, she actually used the word *bone*. I've still not quite recovered from it, which is saying something because she's gotten pretty graphic with me in the past. But there's something about calling it boning that strikes me as hilarious. Maybe I'm more childish than I like to believe.

It's getting late, and I haven't eaten dinner yet. I think I skipped lunch too. A glance at the clock on my laptop explains why my stomach is growling. But that's a good thing because it means I've been absorbed in my work. Which means I'm on the right track—finally. I'm not sitting and staring at the blank page anymore.

It's around eight o'clock by the time I throw together a quick salad and sit down in front of the laptop again. I always work best at night; I have no idea why. I've just never been one of those people who can bounce out of bed before dawn and start working right away. I guess we all have our own rhythms and peculiarities. Lord knows I have my share of them.

When the phone rings, I almost don't even want to look at it. My friends know it's better to text than to call—really, only Maggie and Lois, my agent, bother calling—so it can't be anybody I know or feel like talking to on a Monday night.

I don't know the number that comes up either, so I use my super-sleuthing skills to do a quick reverse search on it while the phone is still ringing.

And I almost drop my salad on the floor when it turns out the call is coming from The Plaza Hotel. And who do I know in the city who's staying at a hotel right now?

"Hello? Hello, hello?" I hope I didn't miss him.

I hear a snicker on the other end. "I was starting to think you were ignoring me." There's that voice of his.

I'm shaking all of a sudden. I honestly never imagined he would call me again.

"I didn't have a number in my phone for you. What, you think I answer the phone for just anybody?"

He laughs. "Good point. I know I don't. How've you been?"

How have I been? I take a look around me, at the many empty cups I've used throughout the day for water and tea. The scratchpad next to my laptop is covered in scribbles, I can't remember if I brushed my hair after taking a shower, and I'm just now shoving a salad into my mouth after having missed lunch.

"Pretty good, all things considered. How about you?"

This is the inanest conversation I've ever had. We're talking to each other like a couple of people who didn't make out in the backseat of a cab, like one of us didn't turn the other one down when they offered sex.

"I'm actually doing really well right now. I have a show tonight, another one of those small clubs like the one you saw me at on Friday. But it's a big deal for me since my agent convinced a handful of music writers to be there, so they can write about it. This could be a turning point for the tour. It would mean a lot if you could make it out. The show starts at nine."

Once again, I almost drop the salad bowl. "Nine?"

"Short notice, I know. But come on. It'll be fun. Afterward, we'll go out for a real, actual date—if you're interested."

The man knows how to sweeten the deal for sure. My heart takes off triple time, and before I know it, I'm halfway to my bedroom, so I can tear through my closet and decide I hate everything I own. "If I'm interested?" I ask with a shaky laugh. "Here I was, thinking you wouldn't be interested anymore."

"Nothing could be further from the truth. I really mean that. The only reason I didn't call before tonight was that I was a little embarrassed, and I figured you didn't think too highly of me. Sometimes, I forget not all women are the same, and I end up asking a question without thinking about it. It's like a knee-jerk reaction, you know?"

"I get it."

"Because I wouldn't have asked otherwise."

And now, I feel worse than before. "I don't think that's the compliment you mean it to be."

Instead of taking it personally, he laughs. "You know what I mean!"

I do, and I love his sense of humor. He gets it. He doesn't take himself too seriously.

"You don't have to apologize to me." Meanwhile, I have him on speaker while I'm texting Hayley. *OMG! He invited me out again. To another show. 45 minutes. Oh my God.*

"I feel like I do though. I already knew by then that you weren't that girl. And I don't want you to be. I want you to be somebody I can get to know, not just another face I'll forget by morning. And that's why I really want to go out with you tonight. Please say you will."

I feel like I shouldn't be too eager, like I should at least make an attempt to sound like I have a life. I mean, nobody who knows me would make the mistake of thinking I have a life, but he doesn't need to know that. "It is sort of short notice …" I hedge, completely pretending even though I'm narrowing down my choice of outfit as I speak. "But I think I can manage it."

"That's awesome!"

Is he only pretending to be as excited as he sounds? Gosh, I really hope not. I don't know why I want so badly for him to be the real deal, but I do. Maybe there's still some part of me that wants him to be the sweetheart he always seemed to be back in the day. No matter how old I get or how mature I tell myself I need to be, there are some things that are practically impossible to let go of.

Just then, a text comes in from Hayley. *OMG! And of course, now, I have the time to go! Why do these things always happen to me?*

Okay, she's starting to sound a lot like me, and now I understand why she loses her patience sometimes.

"Hey, I have a question. I hope this isn't a total bummer, but I feel bad." I explain the situation with Hayley, how she was the one who scored the tickets for Friday and how she was supposed to be the one to introduce us. "I would feel like the world's biggest jerk if I didn't at least ask if she could come with me to the show. We can hang out alone together afterward, but I know she would just die for the chance to meet you."

"Sure! You said she knows Todd?" His agent, I'm guessing since I never learned the guy's name.

"She works with the lawyers who work with Todd," I explain. "She'll probably be a partner there someday, but right now, she's the associate who stays late at night and misses once-in-a-lifetime opportunities, like meeting somebody she's admired for a long time."

"Now that you put it that way, she'd better come."

"That's really sweet of you."

"Hey, why not? One more fan of my music is never a bad thing. And if she's important to you, that means she's probably a pretty cool person. I don't know you very well yet, Kitty Valentine, but you don't seem like the sort of person who puts up with idiots."

Little does he know just what I've put up with in my life, but I'll take a compliment when it's handed to me like that.

"You're the best. I'll let her know, and we'll try to be there before the show starts."

"You'll have the table right up front, just like on Friday. And, Kitty?" His voice lowers, almost to a whisper. "I'm really looking forward to seeing you again. I hope it doesn't sound pathetic, but I thought about you all weekend."

How am I supposed to function when he says something like that?

"You'd better let me go, so I can get ready," I croak since I can't draw in enough air to do anything more than that. He definitely has a way about him. "Text me the address."

Then, I text Hayley. *Show starts at 9. I'll send you the address. Look hot.*

Chapter Twelve

"OH MY GOD. Oh my God. I can't believe we're here."

I have to do a double take. *Is this my best friend? Miss Too Cool for School? Miss Can Have Any Man She Wants But, Damn It, She Wants Lots of Other Things Too?*

And let's not even get started with how flippant and dismissive she was of him during our brunch. It's like she didn't believe a word she said—or she forgot all about it once the prospect of meeting him became a reality.

"Are you for real freaking out, or are you only doing this to mess with my head?" I ask as we take our seats at the front of the room, up by the stage.

Okay, maybe the word *stage* is a bit generous. It's a slightly raised platform with just enough room for a mic stand, a few amps, a stool, and a guitar stand. The entire space is less than what he had on Friday night, and I thought that was too small.

Hayley doesn't seem to mind. Her eyes have practically turned into hearts, like a walking, talking emoji. "I'm for real freaking out. Why would I lie about this? This is, like, a dream come true."

"For a version of you that existed ten years ago, right?"

"Whatever," she snaps, a little huffy. "There's no time limit on making dreams come true, Kitty. Christ."

"I'm just trying to make sure you know how you sound right now. Are you sure you're not running a fever?"

"Considering you're the one he asked on an official date tonight, you sound pretty snarky about me being into this whole thing. Shouldn't you be, I don't know … proud of your man?"

She tosses her hair over both shoulders and tries to look cool, but it's a little too late for that. I know her. I know she's not as cool as she looks. But if I were just walking into this club and seeing her for the first time, I'd chalk her up as a hopeless fangirl who needs a sense of perspective in her life.

"He's not my man, remember? He asked me on a real date tonight, which will make this the second time we've ever hung out together. That's it. This is a casual, no-strings-attached deal. And come on." I look around a little. The place is very dark—no surprise there really—and a little cramped. Sort of dingy. Our table is wobbly and scratched, and the chairs are dirty. "Take a look at this place. I guess he fell further than we thought."

"He's trying to revive his career. Is it a little sadder than you described at brunch? Yes. But I only give him credit for starting at the bottom and working his way up. I mean"—she leans in, lowering her voice to a whisper—"it can't be easy, being thought of as a has-been. People think he's a joke, which he isn't. Poor guy."

"You need to get a little perspective," I whisper, patting her hand. "You really do. Listen, I think this is cool and all, but you've gotta admit, this isn't the super-important gig he was making it sound like when he invited me—or us. I'm pretty sure that dude in the corner is throwing up."

Even Hayley wrinkles her nose at this. "Oh. Okay, well, yeah. Not ideal. But he won't be down like this for long. And he'll have you to encourage him."

I have to wave a hand in front of her face because this is so totally unlike her. "Earth to Hayley. Did the pod people come and replace you? Is the real Hayley frozen somewhere or dead or something? I don't know what the pod people did to the originals they replaced. I don't think they covered that in the movie."

"You're the worst." She orders two martinis from a passing employee, who looks at her like there's no such thing as a martini and we've been imagining drinking them together for years.

"Two of whatever you have on tap," I offer instead, and the girl rolls her heavily lined eyes and walks away. Turning to Hayley, I mutter out of the corner of my mouth, "Something tells me this isn't a martini sort of joint. Beer or whiskey. I figured beer was safest." Hopefully, the glasses are clean.

She's still too busy freaking out to care much. "Don't tell me you weren't as excited as this when you went to see him on Friday."

If she pats her hair or checks her makeup one more time, I might suggest sitting at separate tables.

"Yeah, but I've already told you so much about him, and you reminded me of the many, many people he's probably slept with. I thought he would've lost a little bit of his shine by now."

Her eyes narrow to slits. "Don't rob me of this experience."

"You're right. This is a big deal for you, and I should let you have it."

And if she thinks I'm not going to take deep joy in rubbing this in her face for at least the next ten years …

The lights go down.

Actually, they go completely out.

"What the hell?" Hayley asks along with everybody else in the room.

A spotlight comes up, trained on the stage. Dustin steps into it, smiling, and everybody applauds—quietly and sporadically though since the rest of the room is still pitch-dark, and there are servers walking around and probably taking their lives in their hands. Let's just say, the crowd's not as into seeing him take a seat as they were on Friday.

"Uh, hi. Thank you for being here with me." He looks around, shielding his eyes from the spotlight. "Can we bring the lights up a little, so people can see where they're going in the dark?" As he says it, I'm pretty sure I hear somebody slip in what was probably puke in the corner.

I'm shriveling in my chair. This is a disaster, and he has yet to sing a note. Hayley squeezes my arm.

At least, I think it's her. How would I know? It's so stinking dark in here.

Whoever's in charge of these things turns the lights on, earning them applause. Dustin applauds too.

"Thank you. Now, let's get back to the reason we're here, right?"

I'm proud of how well he's handling this. Sure, we've spent a few hours together, and we have yet to go on an actual date, but I can't help feeling a little protective of him. Like we have a bond, a special secret only shared by us.

"Play 'Falling for You'!"

"Oh no." I hold my head in my hands as yet another heckler insists on giving Dustin the same grief he got on Friday. It's a woman this time, sitting not far from Hayley and me.

"I'm not allowed to play that." Dustin gives a lopsided grin. "Sorry if that's what you came for, but I'm not part of the group anymore. We broke up a long time ago. If you're disappointed, I'm really sorry." He's sweet, apologetic, shrugging it off.

That's clearly not good enough.

"I'm outta here." And she means it, gathering her things, shooting dirty looks at the stage. The entire time she's getting ready to leave, she mutters loudly about has-beens and people who think they're still relevant after so many years. It's pretty harsh.

And my heart breaks for him. He's doing a good job of acting like it doesn't bother him, but it has to. Doesn't it? Nobody would ever know as he launches into his opening song, which sounds just as good as it did when I first heard it.

It's okay for me to create something from scratch in the privacy of my apartment. Sure, it stings like a mother when Maggie comes back with edits on work I am proud of and feel is perfect the way it is. But I can get over it in private and work on it and give it back, and that's it.

I don't have to bare my soul over and over, performing the work of my heart so people can either applaud or boo. So they can ask why I'm not repeating the same tired work I wrote years ago and then get up and leave when I tell them those days are past and I'm trying something new. Something of my own.

"He's really brave," I tell Hayley when the song's over and we're applauding.

Aside from that single heckler, it seems everybody else is glad to be here. What a relief.

"Brave?" She manages to tear her eyes away

from him long enough to remember I'm sitting with her. "What do you mean?"

Maybe she wouldn't understand, and it's too much to explain before the next song starts up. I don't want to be rude—besides, she wouldn't hear a word of it. She's completely wrapped up in Dustin and his music, practically hanging on every word.

Just like everybody else in the room.

I glance around, observing them—I have the luxury of being able to do that since this is the second time I've seen him perform and it's not so new and shiny anymore. They're all hooked, just like I was from the first moment he started to play. There's something special about him, almost magical.

Or maybe it's just my hormones doing the thinking for me.

If it is, I'm definitely not the only one.

And he specifically called to ask me to come to the show. Me! I want to stand on the table and proclaim it to everybody who's so rapturously lost in the music. They can go home and fantasize about him all they want, but I'm the one he'll be going out with after the show.

And to think, I even turned him down on Friday night. I feel like I deserve an award for that.

For once, Kitty Valentine made the right decision, and it looks like it's going to pay off.

"Do I look okay?" Hayley smooths down her hair and then runs her hands over her dress.

It's tight enough that I'm amazed she can breathe. No wonder she seems so giddy and breathless. She's literally suffocating.

"You could wear a bedspread and still look gorgeous, and you know it." All I can do is smile benevolently at her since I'm so cool and experienced now. I already went through all the giggling and blushing and tripping over my tongue on Friday. I'm a veteran of this sort of situation.

For once, I'm the one with the luxury of laughing at her. Lovingly, of course. Always with love. At least, I like to think that's how she feels when she's laughing at me.

She winces, turning away from the wall. "What is taking so long? I think an entire family of rats just ran along the wall over there."

We both pick up our feet and put them on empty chairs, just in case any rodents decide to come over and say hi.

We're still sitting by the stage, and by now, the

rest of the audience has left after fighting for selfies and autographs. Who still collects autographs these days? It took ages for everybody to have their turn with Dustin being kind and generous through what must've been an ordeal.

I'm pretty sure I saw a pregnant woman wearing a wedding ring grab his butt, but there were a lot of people around at the time, so I might be wrong. What is it about him that makes women lose their minds? Hayley's practically ready to burst out of her skin. I've never seen her like this in all the years we've been friends.

Dustin is now chatting with one of the music writers who made it to the show. I don't know if he's the only one who showed up or not. I imagine he'll tell me all about it since he made it sound like such a big deal over the phone.

I'm a professional writer. I know the power of a few complimentary reviews. My fingers are crossed so hard for him, they hurt.

"This is a huge deal. If he can get music writers to review his performances, people might start looking at him as more than just some guy who used to be famous."

"Well, he sounded fantastic." I swear, the girl is ready to swoon. It's a shame I didn't bring smelling salts. "I didn't know he had such a beautiful voice."

"Even after listening to him so many times?"

"As a grown-up, I mean. It's not easy for a teenage singer to maintain their voice into adulthood."

"I didn't know you were such an expert." I nudge her with one elbow, grinning. "Did you do a little research last week and not tell me about it? When we were getting ready to see him on Friday, maybe you looked up other former teen superstars to see how they turned out later on?"

She groans softly, giving me a death look. "Can you not make me sound like such a loser?"

"I'm not. If you think you sound like a loser, maybe it's because you actually are one." I have to duck when she throws a balled-up napkin at me.

"I wanted to prepare myself for possible disappointment. Is that so wrong?"

"No. In fact, I'd have been surprised if you hadn't done that."

Hayley is very much the sort of person who memorizes a restaurant menu long before visiting and then cross-references each dish against recent reviews, so she'll know exactly what's worth trying. I can always count on her for recommendations based on the research she's already done.

Besides, it's not like I didn't do exactly what I just described, looking up old singers and seeing whether they managed to sound as good years after the fact. Spoiler: many did not.

Dustin turns away from the writer after shaking his hand.

"Here he comes," I whisper, and I have to hide a laugh behind my hand when she suddenly sits up a lot straighter, wiping her hands on her thighs the way I did to get rid of the nervous sweat.

When he gets closer to us, I can see the concern etched on his face. It's in the lines on his forehead, the crinkles at the corners of his eyes. His slightly downturned mouth. But it might all be in my head because, in an instant, all that melts away, and he's smiling wide as Hayley somehow manages to find her feet.

"It's such an honor to meet you." Her smile is huge enough that I can almost see her back teeth. When he touches her hand, she giggles in a way I've never heard before from her.

Oh, I really wish I were recording this. I would love to play it back for her every time she acts all cool after I've made a fool of myself.

"Any friend of Kitty's." He smiles. "How did you like the show?"

"Oh, we loved it!" she gushes. "It was so nice of you to have me here tonight. I was devastated at not being able to see you on Friday."

"You can thank your friend for that." He winks at her before turning to me. "She was in a hurry to get here, but she still thought of you."

"What can I say? I'm a saint."

I also might just as well not be here because Hayley has eyes for nobody but him.

"I just, you know, I think it's really brave of you to get up there and perform. It's brave of anybody to do it but especially somebody from your background."

Brave? Okay, now, she's straight-up stealing from me. The nerve!

"Brave? How so?" he asks, looking from Hayley to me with his brows lifted.

I don't think she understands how insulting her observation might seem.

Which is why I clear my throat and step in for her—though honestly, I should let her stew for a little while since she totally parroted what I said earlier and she deserves it, the dork. "You're going into this, knowing people expect you to be a certain way and knowing you can't be that way, but you're still gracious and smiling and willing to perform something special for them. No performer knows how their work is going to be received, but you're brave enough to go out there and share part of yourself with people who might or might not even deserve to have you share with them in such a profound way."

"Yes," Hayley agrees, her head bobbing up and down. "What she said."

He chuckles a little, glancing at me before turning his gaze to Hayley. "That's a really beautiful observation. Thank you."

Even in the room's dim lighting, it's clear she's blushing to the roots of her hair.

"I'm just really impressed with you," she babbles. "And I'm sure you'll be back on top in no time."

Is this what I sound like when my mouth runs away

from me and I'm not making sense anymore? I elbow her as gently as I can and hope she takes the hint. It's like she completely forgot how to behave in public.

"Did you want to go back to your dressing room and freshen up or something?" I offer since somebody has to stop the bleeding and it might as well be me.

Dustin nods, eyes widening. Like he's relieved I changed the subject. "Yeah, let me do that. Hayley, it was a real pleasure meeting you. Thank you for coming out last minute like this and then waiting around to talk with me."

"It's been such a thrill. You don't have to thank me. I should be the one thanking you!"

"Okay," I murmur through clenched teeth.

She finally takes the hint and stands down, clamping her mouth shut until I can hardly see her lips anymore. Dustin pats her on the shoulder before moving past us and through a narrow door leading backstage.

Hayley promptly slumps against the table the second he's away from us. "Oh my God. Did I just make the biggest fool of myself or what?"

"Do I have to answer that question?"

"I think I blacked out for a second there. Did I actually say he was brave? Why did I say that?"

"Because I said it earlier, remember? You totally stole that from me."

"Ugh. He thinks I'm a loser." She stares at the

door Dustin just walked through. "I can tell."

"Probably."

Her head snaps around. "Why didn't you stop me?"

"I tried! And it worked, right? You would still be talking right now if I hadn't stopped you."

"Could you not remind me? Damn it, I'm such an idiot."

"Who cares what he thinks?"

She shoots me a look.

"Besides, I'm sure he doesn't think that," I add. "He's been down-to-earth with me. And he's been dealing with people falling all over him for years. Don't worry about it."

"Easy for you to say. You're the one he wants to go out with later."

I hook a finger under her chin, tilting her face in my direction. "Are you pouting?"

"No."

"You are!" I don't even know what to think about this. It seems so completely outside the norm.

She shrugs, chewing her lip. "It's not easy, meeting somebody you had a crush on for so long and feeling like you're just another tongue-tied fan."

I feel so sorry for her; I have to give her a hug. "It's okay. Really. I'm sure he remembers you the way everybody you ever meet remembers you. As being beautiful and put together and dazzling."

"You're just saying that."

I have to laugh. "I've been standing on the outside for years, sweetie. I've had the enjoyment of watching how people react to you—men especially. You have an effect on them; you always have. So, for once, you got a little tongue-tied. It was bound to happen someday, right?"

"Just do me a favor," she begs. She even folds her hands like she's praying. "If he says anything about me, be nice."

"Why wouldn't I? Gosh, are you okay?" I have to reach out and touch her forehead, just in case she actually is sick. I wondered for a minute, but now, I'm truly concerned.

The girl could take out her phone right now and call up at least ten men who would gladly part with a vital organ for the opportunity to spend time alone with her, but she's losing her mind over this silly situation.

"I'm fine. Sorry. It's like I'm fourteen all over again and I haven't gotten my braces off yet and my skin is all spotty." She even pats her cheeks like she's afraid pimples popped out in the last few minutes.

"He tends to do that to people," I murmur. "Believe me, I can relate."

"I'd better get out of here before I do anything else I'll never stop kicking myself over." She pulls on her jacket, shaking her head and muttering to herself. "One opportunity to meet somebody, and I go and act like today's my first day out in public. Ever."

Boy, for all these years, I've wondered if there was anybody or any situation that could possibly knock her off her game. She's always so on top of things, always in control. The girl barely breaks a sweat in the middle of a heat wave; she's so cool.

All it took was meeting someone who'd meant a lot to her back when she had acne and braces. I guess when push comes to shove, most of us are still those kids, hiding behind makeup and degrees and job titles. Certain situations put us all on the same level. Meeting a childhood hero is one of those situations.

I really need to write about this in my book.

I'm taking notes on my phone when Dustin emerges, and I look up with a smile when I hear him walking my way. It seemed like he was in a pretty good mood when we were chatting, so I guess things went well with the writer. What does he have in mind now? Being in a good mood, after a successful show, I can just imagine what he might want to do to keep the good times rolling.

Only he's frowning again, just the way I thought he was when I first saw him a few minutes ago. And this time, there's no Hayley around for him to perform for. There's just me, and he clearly feels comfortable enough with me now to let the truth slip out.

"That was one of the worst performances I've ever given, and all I want now is a stiff drink." He's already on his way past me, out the door to the street, by the time my feet catch up with my brain and I hurry behind him.

So much for letting the good times roll.

Chapter Fourteen

"I KNOW HOW out of touch this is going to sound." I lean in across the table, pushing aside two empty glasses. His glasses which once contained whiskey. He's on his third already, and I don't think we've been at this bar for more than twenty minutes.

He's good and determined to drink himself into a stupor tonight.

And here I am, feeling like maybe I should've gone home. He's not in any mood for company even though he's insisted that he wants to be with me.

He looks at me finally, having stared down into his glass ever since our server left it for him. Poor thing. It was pretty obvious she wanted to catch his eye, to flirt a little, but he's not in the mood.

"I'm sorry, but I don't understand why you think tonight was such a bad performance."

He rolls his eyes.

"I really don't," I add. "You sounded great to me! The audience was thrilled to pieces. They had nothing but good things to say afterward."

"Were we at the same club? Because from where

I sat, the audience had zero energy. One of them straight-up walked out, Kitty."

"So what? It was just one person, and she was being a total bitch about it. And let me tell you, I never use that word, but I think she qualifies. I hope she's embarrassed by how rude she was."

"You're really too much." He snorts. "You live in this world where people are actually nice to each other. Where they respect each other."

"Excuse me, but that is the world I live in. Where people are supposed to respect each other. Some people are going to be jerks. It is what it is. I stopped reading my reviews a long time ago because I knew they would never do me any good. They would only make me question myself. Believe me, I know how nasty people can be. But that doesn't mean all people are like that, and it doesn't mean your entire performance was a waste because one person was an idiot."

"Unless you've been walked out on, you don't know what I'm talking about." He swirls the whiskey in his glass, snickering. "Trust me, that writer was paying attention. He'll write about that part."

"Yeah, I'm sure they were paying attention to how that situation reflected a lot more on the person who did the walking out than it did on you. You didn't even let it faze you. It wasn't your fault! And it doesn't erase all the people who were clapping and cheering for you by the time the night was over."

"You'd be surprised what some people remember. That writer's going to remember that, and he's going to mention it in his article. I just know he will. Another example of how I'll never escape the past."

I probably shouldn't say this. It's not what he wants to hear right now. At the same time, I'm not sitting here at yet another bar just so I can bolster his spirits. I would do that for Hayley. I might even do it for Matt since he's come through for me more than once.

But Dustin? Aside from some hot making out and the inspiration for my current project, he hasn't given me anything yet that could make up for this.

"I know we don't know each other very well, and I know that until I met you on Friday, I was just another fan. But I feel like somebody has to tell you this."

"I can hardly wait."

Oh, now, he's really going to get it.

"If it wasn't for the past, you wouldn't be sitting here right now."

"Is that right?"

"Yeah, it is. You might want to say good-bye to it, you might want to pretend it didn't happen, and I completely understand and respect that. But it's disingenuous to pretend you don't benefit from people recognizing your name. Because if you were just some guy with some random name nobody had ever heard of, do you think that filthy club would've been packed tonight?"

"Please. That was nothing. I could hand some flyers around the neighborhood and get that many people to come and see me play."

"You really think so? I guess we'll never know, will we? Because the past did happen, and you were an international superstar. And you still have enough name recognition to get gigs like the one you had tonight and for music writers to come out and see you play."

"One." He holds up a single finger. "Todd reached out to half a dozen, and only one showed up. He actually seemed shocked when he said I sounded good. Like he hadn't expected me to."

"Where is this Todd anyway? It seems like your agent would be at your performances, especially when they're supposed to be so important to you. Tonight was supposed to be a big deal, so why wasn't he there?"

"I'm not his only client. Not all of us can get a big deal right out of the gate and earn our agents a lot of money. He's gotta hustle, just like everybody else." He downs his drink and wipes the back of his hand across his mouth while I tell myself that little comment about a big deal wasn't about me—even though I think it was. "I don't even command the entire attention of a manager anymore."

This isn't what I came out for at the last minute on a Monday night. To think, I figured tonight would be exciting and adventurous. Instead, I've been sitting here, watching him throw a pity party. I've thrown enough of those for myself to know he's not about to listen to anything I have to say, any more than I do when Hayley tries to cheer me up.

Which is why I stand up and grab my purse. "If you're going to be this way, I'm going home. I was having a perfectly fine evening before this happened. I'm not going to sit here and let you take your frustration out on me. That's not what I'm here for."

I'm halfway to the door before he gets up to stop me. "Kitty, I'm sorry."

"I really don't want to hear it right now." I'm so furious and so disgusted that I don't care what he has to say.

The night air is cool on my heated cheeks, and I'm thankful for it. It clears my head a little.

Dustin catches up to me halfway down the block. It's amazing he can move as quickly as he does after downing three drinks like they were nothing more than water. "Please, Kitty, I'm sorry. I screwed up."

"Yeah, you did." I turn on him, and there must be something in my face that convinces him how serious I am because he falls back a few steps, like he's surprised. "I'm not one of those people who's going to take whatever you dish out just because you are who you are. You know what I mean? I thought you would know better than that by now. I'm not going to sit by and nod and say, *Yes, Dustin.*

No, Dustin. Because I don't want anything out of you. I thought we were supposed to be getting together for a good time tonight, but here we are. Do you want to be with me right now or not?"

"I do."

"You're not acting like it."

He folds his hands behind his back, taking a deep breath and slowly letting it out. "You're right again. I keep doing all the wrong things. I'm so used to things going a certain way. I can be just as moody and depressing and ignorant as I feel like being, and it doesn't matter because the girl I'm with will put up with anything just as long as she can take a few selfies with me and get a free meal or drinks or a night in my hotel room out of it."

I can't help it. My skin crawls a little bit at the hotel room part. Just how many of these women have there been? Not that it's any of my business. It's just research; that's all.

Yeah, right. That's the ticket. Research.

"I'm not one of those girls!" Okay, maybe that shouldn't have come out so loud. Crap. I hope the people on the other side of the street who have stopped to look don't recognize him. I don't want to be the girl yelling at a onetime international superstar in the middle of the street.

"I know. And the fact that you're still standing here, talking to me, is more than I deserve." He runs his fingers through his hair until it stands almost straight up and then lets out a frustrated growl.

"This is what always ends up happening. I meet somebody worthwhile, somebody like you, and I think, *Great. Finally, a real person. Somebody with, you know, an actual personality and actual interests.* Not to mention, you're smart and successful. You're, like, perfect."

I don't know if I would go that far, though the love-struck teenager still living in some corner of my brain screams and faints.

"Do you really want to be with me right now or not?" I ask again.

"Yes. I mean that. More than anything else." He comes closer, reaching for my hand. His fingertips dance over mine, waking up the nerves and making them sizzle. "And I'm starting to think I need you in my life more than I ever knew before now."

Dang it. The screaming teenager's getting louder, making it difficult for me to think clearly. And I need to think clearly now, especially when his eyes stare so deeply into mine that I'm afraid I'll drown. They are absolutely supernatural, and it's scary how much I love looking into them. I always did—only, back in the day, I was staring at a picture. I had no idea how they looked in a certain light, how much warmth could come from them.

I finally let him take my hand, but I won't give in that easily. "I really want to get to know you better."

"You sure about that? I haven't given you any reason to want to."

"I have good instincts about people—most of the time. And I can tell you're a good person. This has nothing to do with who you used to be back in the day. When you're performing, you connect with people. And they can feel that; they can sense it. It takes a special sort of person to do that."

He slightly shakes his head. "How do you do it?" It comes out almost as a whisper.

"Do what?"

"You look at me, and you see all these different things I never thought were there. You called me an artist the other night. I know it's gonna sound like I have a huge ego, but that's something I haven't been able to forget. It's not every day somebody like me gets called an artist."

"But you are." I tug on his hand. "Come on. Let's walk. It's a beautiful night."

And it is, clear and cool with a crisp breeze blowing down the street. Granted, the breeze carries all the smells of the city, but I wouldn't have it any other way. I'd probably choke if I were ever out in the country or up in the mountains, where the air is truly clean and fresh.

He drapes an arm over my shoulders, and I lean in a little. It's nice, so nice. He's back to being just a normal person again, and that's the version of Dustin I would rather be with right now. Just a man with many hidden depths, capable of writing songs that touch my heart—and not just my heart, but also the hearts of everybody around him.

"I have a confession to make," I murmur as we walk. "I went through a short, dark period not long ago. Work-related. I found out my books weren't selling anymore. And maybe it was too easy at first. I don't know if you did any reading up on me, but I hit the *New York Times* list on my first try. That almost never happens, not unless an author is really lucky and backed by the right people who really believe in their work."

"That's amazing for you."

"It was, and it was amazing the other times too. I live a charmed life. I know that. But I don't think I really appreciated it fully until my sales started slumping. I had been so spoiled." I even laugh softly when I remember that meeting in Maggie's office, where I expected champagne and congratulations and instead was told I needed to start writing steamier books. "Tastes change. The market fluctuates."

"Tell me about it," he groans.

"I had to switch up everything. I couldn't write sweet, cute romance anymore, even when that's all I really want to write. I know you were lashing out earlier when you sort of insulted me. But you made it sound like I'm some mindless Pollyanna who just wants to see the good in everybody and believe we're all in this together and whatever."

"I didn't mean to hurt your feelings, really."

"I think you did a little bit, but it was because you were upset. I get it. You don't have to explain it to me. I know I wasn't feeling very good when my editor pretty much told me that what I was writing was crap. So, I had to spice things up. I had to start following the trends that people wanted to read about, which felt completely foreign to me. I was convinced I couldn't do it, that I would be untrue to myself if I started writing trendier books. I took it personally. Deeply so."

"I'm really sorry that happened." He gives me a small squeeze. "How's it been going since then?"

"You mean, aside from the fact that I'm writing three times faster than I ever used to? It seems to be going well. I adjusted, no matter how much I didn't want to at the time. And it didn't kill me to start writing sexier books. But gosh, I really doubted myself big time. There were moments when I wondered if I should be doing this at all."

"Wow. You and I have more in common than I first thought."

"I know how it feels. And I know how insecurity sucks. When you wonder if you're doing what you're supposed to be doing or if maybe you should consider a career change."

He lets out a low whistle. "This is all I know how to do."

"I truly believe it's what you're meant to do." I stop, turning to him, and I take the chance of sliding my arms around his waist. He pulls me closer. "I really believe you have a gift. I'm not just saying that because I'm standing here in the middle of the sidewalk with you and my teenage self would've killed for this opportunity."

He snickers at this, and his eyes light up. "That's nice to hear."

"You know what I mean. I'm not feeding you a line just because I know it's what you want to hear. I mean it. And I don't have a doubt in the world that you're going to be on top again someday."

He draws me into a deep, long kiss that leaves my legs shaking and my stomach all twisted up in happy, joyful knots.

"I need a lot more of you in my life," he rasps before kissing me again and again until I almost forget we're out in public and there are certain things we probably shouldn't do out here.

So, throwing him to the ground and humping him until I pass out is not an option. But oh boy, do I wish it were.

Because I would like a lot more of him in my life too. Especially if he keeps kissing me the way he is now.

"What are you doing?" I whisper, giggling, as he guides me into a darkened doorway leading up to apartments situated over a corner bodega. "What is this place?"

"Who cares?" he asks before pushing me against the wall, deep in the shadows.

I'm so overwhelmed by this that, at first, there's nothing in the world but Dustin's mouth and hands and his ragged breathing. The smell of sweat and whiskey and cologne, all mixed together in a scent that's entirely his. His knee slides between my thighs before he thrusts his hips against me.

And it's good. It's really, really good.

But it's also a dirty doorway that reeks like pee.

"Dustin, Dustin, wait a sec." I have to remove his hands from my butt when he doesn't listen.

"I need you, Kitty …" He takes one of my hands and places it against the very obvious, very large bulge in his jeans. "This is what you do to me. One kiss, and I'm hard as a rock."

Should I congratulate him? "Can we go someplace a little better than this? Like, where there's privacy?"

He growls softly before pushing away from me. "Damn it. You're making me crazy."

"I'm … sorry? Hey, I'm totally down with this." *Does that sound cool? Or am I trying too hard?* "But not here. In a doorway, where it smells like somebody peed earlier. What happens if someone comes out? Or they want to go in? What if you're recognized? That would be terrible for you."

The man has zero impulse control. He honestly looks pissed that I stopped him. "Yeah, you're right."

"We can go to your hotel, if you want," I suggest, trying to be playful. "Or my apartment."

He opens his mouth to reply—but not before his phone buzzes. "Sorry, hang on." He reads the message and scowls. "Damn it. Todd wants me to meet up with him at some club, so I can talk with some random guitarist he represents."

"Oh, okay. That sounds fun." It doesn't, but I'm trying. I'm really trying.

Even when he gives me a funny, pained sort of look. "I think it's the kind of thing I should do alone. No offense. We'll be talking shop the whole time anyway, so you'd be bored out of your mind."

"Sure. I get it." I'm not upset. Although … "Maybe we can get together later? Or tomorrow? Whenever." *Okay, Kitty, dial it back a notch. You don't have to sound so desperate.*

It's just that I finally made up my mind about whether I'm going to sleep with him or not, and now that I want to, he's not available. *Just my luck.*

"Yeah. That sounds good. I'll have to let you know when I'm free. I've got interviews and stuff all week. But we'll make it work."

Gee, we'll make it work? What are we planning, a business meeting?

I manage a smile as he flags down a cab and even smile through our good-byes.

When I'm in the car, on the other hand, all I can do is fume.

And wonder what he thinks of me if he expected me to do it in a stinky doorway.

Chapter Fifteen

"OH, DEAR. THAT is disappointing."

It's not that I'm surprised my grandmother would say something like that after I announce I'm dating a musician who was once one of the biggest names in the entire world. I expected nothing less from her, being one of those upper-crust ladies who had been born into old money and whose carefully curated world has included some truly spectacular people.

But still, she could have at least pretended to think things over before dumping all over my news.

"What's disappointing?" I press, though I should know better by now.

People shouldn't ask questions they don't really want to hear the answer to, and I know this woman. She won't hold back.

She lowers her fork and knife to her plate—Wedgwood china, naturally, even for something as simple as lunch at home with her granddaughter. "Dear, musicians are never a good choice when it comes to dating. They're too hot and cold, too unpredictable. Too unreliable."

I can't help myself. I know I should try, but I just can't do it. "Strange. It sounds like you're speaking from experience."

She lowers her brow, hitting me with eyes that look a lot like mine. "Watch yourself, Kathryn."

"I'm just saying, how would you know unless you once were involved with a musician? That's all I want to know. You know I would never judge you."

"I'm not entirely sure about that." But there's a twinkle in her eyes in spite of the downward tilt of her lips. Like she wants to frown but can't quite bring herself to do it. "For your information, no, I was never in a relationship with a musician. But I had friends in my youth who were lured by the musicians in the clubs. Jazz musicians mostly."

"Jazz musicians aren't notoriously known for good habits and clean living," I admit. "Not during those days anyway."

"I'm sure not much has changed," she insists.

"He's not that sort of musician though."

She tilts her head to the side, fixing me with a cool stare. "Then, what sort of musician is he?"

"I mean he's, you know, not that sort of person. He's trying to get his career back on track. Can you imagine what that must've been like—being so famous from the time he was a young teenager?"

"Poor baby." She yawns with a roll of her eyes, patting her silver hair into place like it needed any such fixing. She's impeccable, just like always, right down to a fresh manicure and pouty red lips. Somehow, she manages to never leave lipstick on her fork or glass. She's perfect.

"It's true though. He was too young to know what to do, and I guess he couldn't have managed things very well. It was never his, that career. It belonged to the music company. Now, he wants something for himself, and I think that's commendable."

"Indeed. That is commendable." The way she lifts her eyebrows as she picks up her knife and fork that tells me there's something coming, that she's not content to leave it there.

And darn it, I'm right.

"How many women has he slept with?"

"Grandmother!"

"Do you expect me not to care? You tell me you're dating this young man, and he was once incredibly famous. And incredibly young. Incredibly young, incredibly famous people aren't exactly renowned for solid decision-making. I'm sure there were girls throwing themselves at him from the moment he opened his eyes to the moment he closed them—and in between times, if they could manage it."

I can't help but think back to what he told me about the girls who used to hide in his hotel room. "Okay. Sure."

"Do you know he's been safe? Does he have children out there somewhere? These are questions you must ask him."

"I'm not going to ask him that!" My face is hot, burning with embarrassment.

"And why not? Don't you care?"

"Grandmother, this isn't going anywhere. You don't have to worry about anything. I'm a smart person, and I can handle myself. I'm dating him, but there's absolutely no chance of this going any further than that."

Silly me, hoping that would reassure her somehow. All I get for my effort is a shake of her head, the clicking of her tongue.

"I agree, you are a smart girl. But my goodness, do you enjoy telling yourself stories. Perhaps that's what makes you such a compelling author."

"That stings."

"I may have intended for it to sting. There you were, dating a wonderful young doctor—"

"Can we not?" I sigh, looking at the ceiling at the mention of Jake.

"He was the sort of man I would love to see you settle down with. Aside from the fact that he was gorgeous and charming and respectful, he was also dreadfully successful."

"You don't know the first thing about his career."

"He was a doctor."

And I guess that's all she needs to know.

"There are all sorts of people in the world, Grandmother. People have different gifts and talents. I would be terrible as a doctor or even a nurse, but you don't love me any less for that. Unless you do and I've been under the wrong impression my entire life."

"My dear, the only thing about you that has ever disappointed me is your insistence on using that nickname your mother chose."

"I like being called Kitty."

"Kitty is a name for a cat or a burlesque dancer. Not for my granddaughter."

I can't help it. I almost choke on my water, which unfortunately was in my mouth when she made the *burlesque dancer* comment. I have to take my time with swallowing because the impulse to spit out my water and laugh until it hurts is dangerously strong.

Finally, I have myself under control and can offer a snarky comeback. "Hmm. Burlesque dancing. I've never considered that one. Maybe if the whole writing thing doesn't pan out ..."

"I don't find this amusing."

"Funny, but I couldn't tell."

"Kathryn."

"Grandmother. You're taking this way too seriously. I'm dating him. We're not getting married. We're not even seriously dating. It's a casual thing. Once his New York gigs are up, I'm sure he'll move on, and it will all be over."

"And you're all right with that?"

"Why shouldn't I be?"

"You've never struck me as the type to take something like this so lightly."

I roll my eyes.

"Please, don't dismiss me," she urges. "I know you think I'm hopelessly out of touch when it comes to matters such as this, but I assure you, the number of years I have on you doesn't make me an old stick in the mud who's behind the times. They make me wise. They make me aware of the world. I would rather spare you the pain I've witnessed and even gone through myself. I would spare you all of that if I could even though I know it's impossible. We all have to make our own mistakes. Our parents and grandparents can't make them for us. And that is a terrible shame."

She's never come out and said anything like that before. Not to me anyway. We've always been loving but never affectionate, which I guess is what she's comfortable with. Which is what makes what she just said so surprising.

"I know you love me and want what's best for me. But I'm not a little girl anymore. I can handle the realities of the world."

"That isn't what worries me."

"What does worry you then?"

She sighs, and there's genuine pain in her expression. "I don't want to see it harden you. I want you to keep that bright, loving heart of yours. I want you to see good in people. I want you to keep writing romantic stories about love triumphing over everything else. I want you to write it because you believe it, not because someone else tells you that you have to write it. That's what I want. I don't want you to lose yourself to the world, Kathryn."

Well, that was unexpected. So unexpected in fact that when Peter, Grandmother's butler, comes to clear away our plates, I barely acknowledge his presence. It doesn't even occur to me to tell him I'm not finished yet. I'm too overwhelmed.

"And if you happen to marry a doctor and settle down into the sort of life you deserve, so much the better," she adds.

"Do you think that's what's going to happen to me?" *What is it about talking with this woman that leaves me feeling like a little girl again?*

"That you will eventually settle down into the life you deserve? I certainly hope so."

"No, I don't mean that. I mean, what you said before that."

"That the world will harden you? Not if you don't allow it, my dear. And that's the thing so many people don't realize until it's too late—you can choose whether or not to allow yourself to become jaded and cold. You can choose to rail against that too. Some of the happiest, healthiest people I know steadfastly refused to allow the world to change who they are inside."

"What about you?" I can't help myself.

The woman's always been a mystery to me, mostly because she holds herself at a distance. She's regal and cultured, and she was raised way before parents and kids connected and shared and opened up to each other.

She's also filthy and raunchy under that shiny, polished surface. That, I wish she'd keep to herself. But no, she has no problems sharing that part of her personality with me.

"Me?" She lifts her martini glass with a dazzling smile. "I've always marched to my own beat. Don't get me wrong. There have always been parameters to stay within or else I would've risked excommunication from just about every social circle imaginable. While I don't care very much for some of the people in those circles, I know better than to believe myself capable of living without them. There's a reason humans gather together and form their cliques and tribes. We need each other. We can't get along without each other. Your grandfather cared a lot more for appearances than I ever did. When I lost him, I gained a bit of freedom. I know how it sounds, saying something like that. But time has given me the benefit of hindsight." Her smile slips a little by the end.

I believe she was madly in love with my grandfather but just doesn't know how to say it.

"I wish I could find somebody to be madly in love with," I confess, staring at the arrangement of flowers in the center of the table. Enormous, fragrant roses in cream and pink. Her favorite colors.

"You deserve that. You're young. You're beautiful. You have the entire world at your feet. Don't sell yourself short for the sake of a few books, dear."

"But I have to—"

"I know what you have to do—or what that horrid editor of yours wants you to do."

"I can't afford to go unpublished."

"I realize that. How many times have I wished your grandfather had purchased a publishing house?"

"Grandmother." I have to laugh. "I wouldn't accept any offer you handed me. That's cheating."

"As if the world wasn't built on cheating and nepotism." She laughs with me. "I don't want you to lose your sweetness, darling, but there's something to be said for realism."

Soon, she stops laughing, eyeing me again. "Don't waste the best years of your life dating random men for the sake of your career. I wouldn't want to see you regret the wasted time."

Wow. Talk about putting my life into sobering perspective. "If something good comes out of it, the time's not wasted. Right?"

"There's that positive attitude I like to see." But she's still not smiling. If anything, she looks a little sad.

So sad that I feel like I have to cheer her up. "I'm learning more about myself as a person too. When you look at it that way, you'll see what a good thing this is. I holed up in my apartment for years, writing. Just writing. I hadn't had more than a handful of dates in all that time. If anything, I was wasting time then. Now, at least I'm getting out and into life. I'm learning about people. I'm learning about what I will and won't accept from a partner."

"That is important," she agrees.

"If anything, I owe Maggie a lot of gratitude for pushing me out of my comfort zone. Without this shake-up, I might've ended up a recluse, surrounded by all the stray cats I'd have brought in during my rare forays out into the neighborhood."

"Dear, I would never have allowed that to happen. I can accept an eccentric granddaughter. I cannot accept the thought of her living in squalor, surrounded by defecating cats."

"Grandmother."

Chapter Sixteen

"I NEED YOU. Now."

She squirmed against him, thrilled and breathless. He wanted her? Her? Plain, mousy, the girl who had never once stood out in a crowd? When he could have any girl he wanted?

"Me?" she whispered in his ear as he did things to her that turned her legs to jelly.

She had to hold on to him and lean against the wall at her back to stay upright while his tongue flicked over her neck. When he bit down just a little, she gasped.

But it was good. It was so good.

She closed her eyes and let her head fall back against the bricks behind her. He took this as the go-ahead to continue kissing down her neck, to her chest, where he spread her blouse open with his chin and chafed her sensitive skin with the scruff on his jaw.

"So sweet," he rasped, grinding his hard cock against her.

She was a feast, and he was devouring her like a starving man. She threaded her fingers through his hair, lost in sensation and sheer, blinding joy. He wanted her. He wanted her so badly that he'd—

"Wait." She brushed his hand away, the hand crawling up her thigh, the fingers hooking around the lacy hem of her panties. "Hang on."

"I have to have you," he groaned, his breath hot in her face before he thrust his tongue into her mouth, teasing and tormenting.

She whimpered, clutching him tightly, for fear her weakened limbs would no longer hold her up. Her desire for him couldn't be quenched.

But that didn't mean fucking in a filthy alley. She still had standards, no matter how many fantasies a quickie against the wall would fulfill. Because deep down inside, she wanted him to take her. She wanted to be slutty, just once, instead of always being the good girl who did the right thing.

She couldn't give in; that wasn't her. When he felt around again for her panties, she forced herself to ignore the stimulating touch of his fingers against her wet, swollen flesh—God, it had been so long, too long since somebody touched her there—and pushed him away.

WHEW. I HAVE to sit back for a second and take a few deep breaths after writing that.

Because it's one thing to imagine that happening, to build a scene in my head and describe what I'm seeing and what the characters feel in that situation.

It's another to imagine myself as the girl against the wall with her dress hiked up, with Dustin as the man of my dreams, positioned firmly between my thighs. I might need a cool drink before continuing with the scene.

I'm on my way to the kitchen for just that when there's a knock at the door.

"Food's here."

"Oh, great." I open the door to find Matt standing in the hall with a bag in one hand. The other hand is petting Phoebe's head.

"Do you mind if she joins us? She's been a little whiny lately, and I don't know why." He looks down at her, and I can see the concern written in his expression. It's sweet, how much he loves her.

"Of course. She's missing her daddy, I guess. Have you been out a lot lately?" I usher the dog inside the apartment and then her owner.

"No more than usual. I think she likes you, honestly. Always scratching at the front door. Always whimpering next to your door when we go out for walks."

"Really?" I drop to a crouch in front of her, scratching her behind the ears. She's a beauty, and Matt takes excellent care of her. "Do you like me, sweetie? I like you." Even if she once made me sprain my ankle on the stairs.

In the end, if it hadn't been for her, I might never have spoken a single word to Matt. He used to be the astonishingly hot neighbor from across the hall, who I was too nervous around to say anything but a quick hello to in passing.

Now, we sometimes coordinate our food delivery to save on the fees, and more often than not, we end up eating together. Since he works from home the way I do, he knows what it means to feel cut off from the rest of the world. As much of a hassle as it has to be to deal with people day in and day out, like working in an office, my grandmother was right about humans needing each other.

"Iced tea?" I ask from the kitchen as he sets things up in the living room.

"Hmm? Yeah, sure. Thanks." He sounds distracted.

Too distracted.

Oh, shoot.

I look over my shoulder and out through the kitchen to the desk near the window, where I was just working. Where he's now reading what I finished before he showed up. *Shoot, shoot, shoot.*

"Not bad." He throws a wicked grin in my direction. "Not bad at all. You could heat it up a little though. I know that's what your editor and your readers want."

I wish there weren't a telltale flush creeping over my skin right now. "Oh? How would you heat it up?"

Right, because I'm confident and cool and he's not half as intimidating as he used to be. In fact, he doesn't intimidate me at all anymore. He's just the guy who lives across the hall and thinks of me as a sister. No biggie.

Though he's still impossibly handsome and

about to talk sex with me, and who wouldn't blush in this situation? I can't be the only one.

"I'd definitely have him finger her a little," he affirms, nodding. "I mean, he's not gonna keep stroking her thigh or whatever you have him doing with his one hand. If he's forceful and demanding, he's gonna go for it right then and there."

"Oh. Okay." I sure do wish I could stop blushing. I really do.

"So"—he takes a seat on the sofa, smiling that knowing smile of his that I'd like to slap off his face sometimes—"how does the scene end? You have her pushing him away."

"Right." I sit on the floor since even sharing a piece of furniture with him seems like a bad idea right now.

He's feeling naughty, and he knows I'm not exactly comfortable with getting into conversations like this. I might be able to write it—and even then, it still doesn't come naturally to me, hence him needing to coach me along—but talking about it? Yikes.

"What happens next?" He opens a container of chow mein, which he knows I think looks like vomit and which is probably why he always orders it and eats it in front of me. *Slowly*. With great relish.

"I'm not sure. I mean, I know they're not gonna do it."

"Ah, come on."

"Not yet anyway. They will eventually."

"You're still holding back."

"So, you think she should do it right there, in that dirty alleyway? Gross." Then, I remember something he once told me. "But you've done it on the roof of our building, so I guess that wouldn't seem like such a big deal to you."

"Ouch." He doesn't look hurt in the least. In fact, he's smiling—because of course he is. "Would it make you feel better to know it was sort of a romantic experience?"

"No."

"And there were blankets and stuff? And I made sure she was comfortable?"

"Stop."

"You need to live a little, Valentine."

"Sure, sure. But that doesn't mean screwing in an alley where anybody could walk by and God only knows how many diseases are floating around."

"Okay, that I can agree with. But this isn't real life we're talking about. It's supposed to be fantasy. Just because you would tell your rock-star boyfriend to get his hands out of your panties—"

"Not my boyfriend."

"That doesn't mean every woman in the world would. And even if they would, that's probably not what they wanna read about. This is supposed to be escapism, not real life. What do you think a woman reading your book would want to read about? If she were in a dark alley with the rock star she used to dream about and who she probably had feelings for now or whatever." He waves this off like it doesn't matter, which is pretty much on-brand for him. Like, God forbid people have feelings.

"I guess some of them might want to read about a quickie in an alley."

"Of course they would! I mean, come on. That's the whole point of what your editor wants from you now."

"Has she called you? Do you two get together to discuss this?"

"No, but I'd be glad to charge her a consulting fee." He's grinning as he pops a wonton into his mouth. "I'm sure she would agree."

I decide against getting on his case for talking with his mouth full because I know he'd only open his mouth and let the food fall out if I did.

He's right. I hate that he's right. My instincts on this are still all messed up. I keep writing about nice girls, which is fine because there are plenty of nice girls in the world, but I need to be writing about nice girls who go against everything they've ever believed about themselves in favor of something different. Something sexy.

"So … how did your boyfriend react when you turned him down?"

I almost choke on my bean curd. "Excuse me?"

"You heard me. Don't play. The girl in your book was gonna turn her guy down because you turned him down. Right?"

"That's none of your business."

"I have my answer." He sits back with that smug smile of his.

Why do I even bother spending time with him?

"Fine. You're right. But don't tell me I was wrong to do that."

"I absolutely don't think you were wrong to do it. Not even a little bit."

I sit there, waiting for the other shoe to drop, but he doesn't say anything else right away. In fact, he goes back to his food. I should probably let it go, right? We could easily change the subject. I wouldn't have to suffer under the humiliation of him knowing about my sex life.

Or lack thereof.

But I've never done things the easy way.

"Why not?" It sounds casual enough, doesn't it? Especially since I'm picking around in my container of bean curd and mixed vegetables when I ask.

"Because it wasn't right for you. It might be right for some people, but it wasn't for you. I would never imagine you to be the kind of girl who would do something just because it's what somebody else would do. You're just not the one-night-stand type of person. There's nothing wrong with that."

"So, why do you sound dismissive when you say it?"

"I wasn't trying to be dismissive. It's just that some people have it in them to sleep with somebody and move on, and some people don't. If you ask me, there's nothing wrong with either type of person. Don't try to draw me into an argument right now because I'm not trying to argue with you. I'm sitting here, telling you I think you did the right thing."

"For me."

"Who else would you do it for? Not for a book, I would hope."

"No …"

"Besides, the guy's probably crawling with diseases."

"He's not."

"Oh? Did you have him go to the clinic for testing? Or maybe he's already given you a look at his medical records."

"You're one to talk. There's been a parade of women in and out of your apartment ever since you moved in."

"I take care of myself, thank you. And unlike your boyfriend, I wasn't sleeping my way through half the world when I was a teenager."

"Not my boyfriend."

He ignores this. "I can't imagine a kid that age would make a lot of smart choices. So, maybe keep that in mind."

"I'm not a child. I've already kept that in mind."

"Good. Just be careful, you know? I doubt this guy is the type for you to get serious about."

"I never said I was even considering getting serious! You're the one who insists on calling him my boyfriend. I never once did, and I won't because he's not. We're just having fun."

"Apparently not since you keep turning him down."

"Once, genius. I turned him down once." Twice, but he doesn't need to know that either. "Isn't your food getting cold? Shouldn't you eat it and stop talking for a little while?"

Honestly, he's enough to give me a headache.

It seems like I've finally gotten through to him though since he turns his attention to his lunch and the dog who's been waiting patiently for a bite of food all this time. I don't even know how Phoebe puts up with him; I really don't. And she's just a dog.

Still, it's good to hear he thinks I made the right decision. I mean, I know I did, and Hayley agreed with me—sort of.

Somehow, hearing it from Matt eases my mind in a way Hayley didn't. Maybe because he's a man—and a total horndog.

I feel a lot better now. Even if I have to watch him eating chicken chow mein.

Chapter Seventeen

WHEN THE SOUND of Dustin's knock echoes through the apartment, I instantly decide that I hate every piece of furniture I own, that the walls should be repainted, and that I should seriously consider hiring an interior decorator.

But that's just a silly knee-jerk reaction. I have to stop reacting to him that way. He's just a person. The person I invited over because it seems like we haven't been able to sync our schedules up lately and it's been a week since I saw him. He finally has a free night, and I pushed pretty hard to get him to agree to spend it here, at my place. Just the two of us.

Well, he's not going to wait in the hall forever. I fling the door open with a wide smile to find him standing there with a bouquet of roses in one hand and a bottle of wine in the other. He looks perfectly mussed, his hair falling over one eye, the sleeves of his tight sweater pushed up to his elbows to reveal his tattooed forearms.

"Hey, gorgeous." It's practically a purr—or at least, that's how it sounds to me.

Darn it, no matter how many times I tell myself not to react this way, there's still part of me that wants to squeal and shriek and jump around in disbelief. *He's talking to me. I'm gorgeous.*

"Hey, handsome."

I step back to let him come in, and he rewards me with a deep, passionate kiss that leaves me panting and wanting more.

"I've been wanting to do that all week," he whispers, his face only inches from mine. "You have no idea."

"I think I do." I giggle.

If anything, he has no idea how much I've thought of him since I've spent the past week writing about a character based on him.

I leave him to look around a little while I find a vase for the flowers.

"This is beautiful. Really stunning. I love the color on the walls."

Okay, so maybe my decorating instincts aren't as terrible as I thought they were. "Thanks. I've always liked that shade of blue-green. Darker than a Tiffany box, but not too dark."

"Exactly. It's really striking. Bold." He turns to me with a smile and accepts the wine key I hand him.

"Considering that this is the place I spend most of my time, I figured I might as well surround myself with things I like." I watch as he wanders over toward the many, many books lined up along the walls. They're arranged by color now, though I might change that up soon. Probably the next time I get stuck on a scene and look for a way to distract myself from the work I should be doing.

"Well-read too. I guess that goes with the territory." He glances over his shoulder with a grin.

"I bet, in your apartment or your house, there's all kinds of music."

He pours wine into the two glasses I brought out from the kitchen. "I have a music room at my house, out in LA. I miss it right now—which is funny, when you think about it. I can listen to any music imaginable, thanks to the magic device in my pocket."

"But it's not the same as being home with your own collection."

"Not even close." He sits down next to me and touches his glass to mine. "And there is such a huge difference between the vinyl and the digitally remastered versions of so many really great albums. It's like they suck all the soul out of the recording when they mess with it like that."

"I've heard that argument before, but I've never owned a record player or any vinyl albums, so I can't really offer my opinion."

"You don't own a turntable?" He looks downright stunned.

"No. I don't own a girdle either." When he sputters a little, I explain, "It's just that, for most of my life, vinyl records were so old-fashioned. Now, like you said, everything is digital. I can listen to just about anything on my laptop. And I know that's not the same."

"We need to get you a turntable."

"Do we really though?" I ask. All I want to do is spend time with this man, and it seems like he is always coming up with ways to change the subject. "I kind of thought we would spend tonight together …"

"I don't mean right this very minute." His gaze softens along with his voice, which drops into something barely louder than a whisper. "Trust me, I want to spend tonight with you too."

"Good."

This is happening. This is really happening.

I'm not going to play the good girl tonight. No way. Tonight is a night to be bad in the best way possible.

"What did you have in mind?" He settles in, draping an arm over my shoulders and pulling me in until my head is resting against him.

Honestly, this is enough for now. Sitting here, being together, relaxing. I could almost fool myself into imagining that this is our life, the two of us. Enjoying these brief moments together, focusing on each other when we have the chance to. It's all too easy, falling into reverie, a fantasy that will probably never come true.

"I thought maybe we would order something to eat, for starters? If you're hungry, that is. We could watch a movie on my laptop."

"You don't have a TV?" He sounds surprised as he looks around. "I didn't notice that at first."

"I never got around to buying one." I shrug. "Anything I want to watch, I can find online or stream it or whatever. If I had a TV around, I would leave it on all the time and get distracted. I know myself well enough."

"I hate silence." He laughs at himself a little, shrugging. "Little-known fact about me. A silent house or apartment freaks me out."

"We can turn some music on if you want—even though it'll only come from my laptop, and I know that's not nearly good enough." I finish with a wink, standing up from the couch. "Anything you want to hear?"

"I could go for some jazz," he offers.

That's unfortunate since, now, all I can think about is my grandmother's warnings. *Why couldn't he have picked hip-hop or swing music or religious hymns or anything else, literally anything at all?*

"I have to admit, I'm not well-versed in jazz. You might have to tell me a specific artist to look for."

"It seems like I have a lot to teach you."

Why do I get the feeling we're not talking about music anymore?

He comes to me, where I'm standing at my laptop, and takes me by the hips. He presses me against the desk, our bodies flush against each other. "I'd like to start teaching you now," he murmurs, kissing the tip of my nose, my cheeks, my chin. "I mean, I could go for something to eat, but you're much tastier than anything I can imagine being delivered."

What is a girl supposed to say to that besides, "That sounds good to me."

The next thing I know, his hands are under my butt, and he's lifting me, carrying me to the couch with my legs locked around his hips. I can't help giggling as he lowers me, lowering himself at the same time until he's settled between my thighs.

"Lesson number one," he growls, planting tiny kisses on my collarbone. "You are wearing way too much clothing right now."

"We'll have to do something about that," I whisper, closing my eyes and succumbing to the bliss rolling through me in waves as he unbuttons my blouse with one hand while his mouth travels lower, lower …

He stops at the sound of scratching at the front door. I open my eyes to find him looking toward the door, confused.

"What's that?"

Of all times for Phoebe to decide she wants to pay a visit.

"Excuse me. I'm sorry." I manage to slide out from under him, buttoning my shirt and smoothing my hair into place as I go to the door. "She might've gotten out from the apartment across the hall."

He mutters something I don't quite understand, and I don't need to know exactly what he's saying to catch the general idea. Considering I'm throbbing like crazy between my legs, I understand the sentiment.

Sure enough, there's a certain golden retriever sitting at the door.

"Hi, pretty girl." I crouch in front of her, and laugh as she kisses my chin. She probably smells Dustin on me. "Where's your daddy?"

Matt's door is partly open, which is unlike him.

To my surprise, Phoebe starts to growl. I glance over my shoulder to find Dustin walking toward us.

"Don't be rude," I whisper, trying to chide her. "Be a nice girl."

"Phoebe!" Matt throws his door open wide, looking disheveled, wearing nothing but a towel around his waist. He groans when he sees her. "What do you think you're doing?"

"Did you leave the door open?" I sigh, shaking my head. "And you're the one who gets on my case for doing things like that."

Rather than argue with me, which is normally the way this would go, Matt looks into my apartment and finds Dustin standing behind me. "Oh, I'm sorry. Yeah, I guess I didn't close the door all the way. I was about to get in the shower, and I knew something was up when she didn't follow me into the bathroom. I don't think I've taken a shower alone since I adopted her."

He then extends a hand toward Dustin, reaching over my shoulder. "Matt Ryder."

"Dustin Grant." He doesn't sound thrilled, not even a little.

Even when he was in a bad mood and he met Hayley, he managed to sound upbeat and friendly. He knew he was talking to a fan and didn't want to disappoint her.

After sizing Matt up, he's probably decided it's not worth it.

"Oh, right! You're the musician! Kitty told me about you."

The two of them hold each other's gaze, and I might as well not even be present. Frankly, I sort of wish I weren't because I'm getting the feeling they're having a conversation far beyond anything they've said out loud.

"All good things, I hope."

Is there a law that people have to say that? Because I swear, if I had a nickel for every time I heard that …

"Actually, she hasn't had the chance to tell me too much. You two haven't known each other for very long."

I'm about to choke on all the testosterone.

"Anyway," I interject probably a lot louder than I need to, "here's the dog. Try to make sure your front door's closed all the way next time, okay? I wouldn't want to see you lose this sweet girl." I reach down to pet her head, but she's too busy growling softly at Dustin.

"Sorry." Matt shrugs. "She's not usually like this. She's generally friendly to everybody."

Is it my imagination, or did he look at Dustin when he said that?

"She's just jealous that I'm hanging out with somebody who isn't her."

Honestly, if I were wearing a pair of tap shoes, I couldn't dance any harder than I am right now. I'm trying desperately to keep things light and upbeat and to prevent these two from, I don't know, pulling out their penises and measuring them. Or whatever men do in situations like this.

"Nice to meet you," Matt offers through gritted teeth.

Dustin turns away, mumbling, and Matt's eyes widen when they meet mine.

I don't trust him, he mouths.

I didn't ask you, I mouth back, and then I stick my tongue out at him because I am very mature. He's used to that by now anyway.

When it's all over and I close the door, all I can do is put a hand on my forehead. "I'm so sorry about that." I laugh. *Yes, it was just a silly detour. Nothing more serious than that.*

Dustin doesn't appear to share my opinion. "Who is that guy?" He jerks his chin toward the door.

"Just my neighbor. It's not a big deal. I'm sorry if he came off a little too …"

"Macho? Like a complete jerk-off?"

I know I shouldn't come to Matt's defense, but I can't help it. "He's not that bad. He's like a brother. He drives me nuts, but I guess he feels like it's his job to protect me."

He snorts, picking up his wineglass and draining it before pouring more. "Yeah, like a brother. I'm sure that's how he sees you."

I feel like I'm joining a conversation already in progress, and I have no idea what I missed. "What does that mean?"

"Oh, get real. I know you're a nice person and you have a great heart and you're sweet, but let's not kid ourselves. He's obviously after you."

"After me?" I can't help it. I have to laugh. "Hardly. Please, let's not even think about him. He's just my neighbor."

"Does your neighbor come to your door, wearing nothing but a towel all the time?"

"No. Only when he was in the middle of getting into the shower and his dog got out."

Now is definitely not the time to describe our first real meeting—when I took off all my clothes and threw up on Matt's carpet before passing out in his bed. There are certain things Dustin doesn't need to know about, especially when he's looking and sounding as angry as he does right now.

"It just seems a little too convenient to me."

"Considering that you don't know the first thing about my life or the way I live it, Dustin, I don't think you have enough information to decide whether something is convenient or not. And, if this is the way you're going to act, I think tonight was a mistake. I'm sorry things turned out this way, but life happens. Either you can deal with that or you can't."

He picks up the bottle, still half-full, and shrugs. "Whatever. If that's the way you feel about it, I'll be going."

"I guess that's for the best."

I pull the door open for him, and he saunters out into the hallway, throwing a dirty look at Matt's closed door before turning and walking toward the stairs.

Now, how did everything go from wonderful to terrible in no time flat? I mean, this has to be a record, even for me.

Chapter Eighteen

I'M A LITTLE apprehensive, waiting in line to get into Dustin's latest show. There are only four more gigs in the city before he moves on to Boston.

Honestly, I wouldn't even be here if it wasn't for the many bouquets of flowers he sent since our last disastrous almost-date two nights ago. My apartment would make a great venue for a wedding ceremony right now. Roses as far as the eye can see.

What is it with rich guys and roses?

And it isn't just the flowers either. He must've sent at least twenty or thirty texts later that night, apologizing for coming off like such a jerk. We talked things out, and he admitted that he felt jealous and threatened by Matt's presence across the hall.

Needless to say, it took all of my self-control not to respond with two simple words: No duh. It had been pretty obvious to me at the time that he was freaking out because he was jealous and unsure of Matt's place in my life. I might not have a ton of experience with men, but I know what a jealous man looks and sounds like—and I knew at the time there wouldn't be any convincing him otherwise, which was why it was just as well that he left.

But that is in the past. This is now, and I'm waiting in front of the club for the doors to open.

It's so funny. I was just as excited as these women when I first saw Dustin perform. Wondering what he would be like, what he would sound like, even what he would look like now. Remembering all the music from my youth, all the days and nights I'd spent pining for him, listening to his songs and wishing he were singing to me.

And now, here I am. Smiling benevolently at them since I happen to know what it's like to kiss him. To be touched by him, to have him want me. All these poor little peasants can live in their dream worlds. I know what it's really like to spend time alone with him.

I have to admit, I'd like to know a lot more about spending time with him. It seems like something always gets in the way. Either my stupid principles or a certain golden retriever who lives across the hall.

I'm starting to wonder if we're ever going to get the chance to take this to the next level before he's out of town. Maybe it's just not meant to be. Maybe I was only ever meant to be a quick hook-up while he's in town.

And I need to be okay with that.

Am I okay with that?

Before I know it, we're moving into the room

where he'll be performing. This is much nicer than where I've seen him perform before. He told me that since things are going so well and he's been getting great feedback and reviews, his agent was able to talk some of these club owners into giving him bigger rooms and more tickets. It's still a far cry from where he used to be, but I can already see how his situation is improving.

It won't be long before he's right back up on top. I'm sure of it. And I can't help but glow with pride as I take my seat at the front of the room—at a table reserved for me.

"Why does she get to sit up front? There aren't supposed to be reserved tables here," one of the women at a nearby table asks this question to no one in particular, raising her voice loud enough for me to hear it. "We waited outside for two hours to get in first, and we're not allowed to have the best seats?"

"Maybe she's his girlfriend," somebody else suggests.

I try to pretend I can't hear the way they snicker and whisper. Let them whisper. Wouldn't they feel stupid if they knew the truth? That I'm not just obsessing over the past. That the man's tongue has been in my mouth, for God's sake.

I have to admit to myself, if to no one else, that dating him full-time would be a full-time job, point-blank. I don't know if my self-esteem could handle it, any more than I could handle the idea of thousands or even millions of women lusting after my man. If I've learned nothing else from this experience, I've learned that much.

I doubt Maggie would care about the personal lessons I'm learning, however. She wants a book out of this, a book which I'm slowly but surely putting together. Maybe when this is all over and I stop dating for the sake of my writing, I can write a memoir about all the different men I dated and how they all taught me a lesson or two.

Depending on how long this experiment of mine lasts, it could be a pretty epic collection of stories. Good thing I've been taking notes all along.

When the lights go down, that familiar rush of energy hits me from all sides, and I have to smile. Yes, he can be an insufferable jerk, but I'm proud of him. He's insecure, just like everybody else in the world. There's another lesson brought to life: it doesn't matter how popular a person is or how much success they've seen in the past; we are all just trying to get by, and there will always be insecurities we can't let go of.

Because really, at the end of the day, there's no comparison between Dustin and Matt. At least, not on paper. Sure, Matt probably makes good money doing what he does, and of course he's hot. Women must find him sexy because Lord knows he's successful enough with them.

But Dustin? He's got that magic, the charisma that oozes from him the second he takes his seat and smiles out at the audience. The man sparkles and smolders at the same time; it's like he's not even human.

I wish there were a way I could describe the sound of dozens of pairs of panties melting all at once because I would love to put it in a book.

"Hi, everybody. Thank you so much for being here with me tonight. It's so good to see you and know I have fans like you out in the world."

There's that indescribable sound again. I'm surprised there are any panties left to melt at this point.

"It means the world to me that you care enough to be here. I hope I make it worth your time."

They're eating out of the palm of his hand. And he knows it. I have to commend him; he's getting better at working the small crowds with each show. As good as he was at first a couple of weeks back, it was nothing compared to now.

I'm familiar enough with the music to follow along—at least, until he surprises me at the end of the first set.

"This next song is very new. So new that I just wrote it in the last few days. You'll be the first people to hear it performed."

He scans the room, finally landing on me with a grin. "It's for somebody special who was kind and patient enough to be here tonight. I'm not an easy guy to get along with, but she's one of the good ones, and she has come out to support me anyway."

I'm dying. I am dying where I sit. They'll have

to come with a body bag to take me away because there's no way I'm walking out of this club at the end of the show.

I can think of worse ways to go.

He strums across the strings, humming softly before launching into the lyrics. *"She's there with a smile when the world has turned its back. She'll stand up to me when I'm on the attack. There are times when she sees me, and I want to hide. She doesn't deserve the hurt that's inside ..."*

RIP, Kitty Valentine. I mean, I'm basically a puddle at this point.

The best part though? The very best part? That is when the song is over and the audience applauds and I can just feel those women from that nearby table staring at me. Especially when Dustin looks at me again and smiles, and I smile back, completely overwhelmed and emotional.

There's still that tiny, petty part of me that's glad they heard that and glad they know it was about me.

No. I could not handle being this man's girlfriend. No way. I don't even know if I'd like myself very much after a while.

The second he leaves the stage for his fifteen-minute break, I'm surrounded by at least seven or eight women.

"Are you dating him?"

"Oh my God, how did you meet? What was it like?"

"What's it like, being with him?"

"Oh my God, if he sang a song about me, I'd die."

"Okay, all right, enough." A tall, dark-haired man I don't recognize shoos them all away and rolls his eyes once they wander off and leave us alone together. He's wearing a suit jacket, a tailored shirt, jeans. Nice but casual. And not the sort of person I'm used to seeing at these shows.

Usually it's just groupies wearing Crazy 4 You T-shirts.

"Uh, thanks?" I manage.

He even sits down, which strikes me as being a little forward, but I'm too grateful to him just now to care very much about what he chooses to do.

"I'm Todd Everett." He extends a hand, and I nod in understanding as we shake.

"You're Dustin's agent."

"Guilty as charged. And you're the girl he wrote that song about. He's been talking a lot about you. I'm glad I finally got the chance to put a face to the name."

I feel like there's something I should say, something positive. "This is nice." I gesture around me to the room, which is a far cry from that dingy little basement where some random guy threw up in the corner and their idea of dimming the lights was turning them out completely. "I can tell that you must really be hustling to get him in front of people."

"Name recognition helps." He shrugs, leaning back in his chair. "I have to admit, I didn't recognize your name the first time I heard it. I had to do some digging."

Somehow, this strikes me as funny, though he doesn't chuckle when I do. In fact, he looks downright annoyed.

"Digging?" What could that possibly mean?

"He explained to me the connection, why you went to see him in the first place. My lawyer. Your friend at the law firm."

"Oh, sure." For some reason, the hair on the back of my neck is standing up, and I feel slightly sweaty.

Something's not right here. This person doesn't like me, and I don't know why. I've never been very good at dealing with people who don't like me.

"I did a little asking around. So, you're writing a book about him and didn't think we'd find out, huh?"

And there it is. I imagine it's something akin to the feeling of being on an elevator and having it suddenly drop or going down the first hill on a roller coaster. My stomach sinks until I'm pretty sure it's left my body.

I have to be careful to keep my voice low as I lean closer to him. "No, I'm not writing a book about him. Where did you get that idea from?"

"From my contacts at the firm. I know what you do for a living."

"So does Dustin."

"I know. We're both aware of what you're doing."

"Hold on a second." *Was I not just riding high, like, less than a minute ago? How did everything turn around so quickly?* "I think some wires might've gotten crossed here. I'm not writing a book about Dustin. Not at all. Anything I write is completely fictional. Now, am I writing a character with the same career as Dustin? Yes, I am. But not once is his name mentioned, not the group, not even the city we're in right now. None of that."

All of a sudden, he smiles, and it's like I might as well be sitting across from a different person. "I don't think you understand. I'm not saying that's a bad thing. In fact, it would be great for his brand if a romance novel involving him came out in the next month or so."

He might as well have started speaking in a different language.

"I don't think you understand, with all due respect. Like I just said, the book doesn't directly involve him. I like Dustin a lot, I love spending time with him, and the characters in my book will go through slightly similar situations to what I've observed while I've been with him. You know, what it's like for him to be swarmed by fans, who expect somebody from the past, not who he is right now. That sort of thing."

"So, you'll never mention his name?"

"No! Not at all. I've done everything I can to separate the two of them. My character and him, I mean."

"Okay. So, what? His name will be used for promotion? Based on the relationship between you and him, I mean."

What is this guy not getting?

"No. And honestly, I would think a lawyer would have told you that. I'm not allowed to use him that way."

"Let me understand." He props his elbows on the table, folding his hands under his chin.

I don't like this guy. I really don't like him.

"You were using your experiences with my client to write a book that you hope is going to sell all these copies or whatever. But he doesn't get anything out of it. Not even a name drop on a promotional tour?"

"For one thing, I don't do promotional tours." I shrug. "For another thing, you're making it sound like I'm some sort of mercenary or something when nothing could be further from the truth. I really like Dustin. I'm not trying to use him to sell more copies, if that's what you're worried about."

"What I'm worried about is him not getting anything out of this. Why don't you understand? Or are you deliberately playing dumb?"

"Are you serious? I thought he and I were seeing each other. I didn't think he wanted to get anything out of it but spending time with me, getting to know me."

He blinks hard, like he doesn't understand. "Do you really think he's hanging around you because you're such a sweet person? You don't think there are hundreds of other women he could be with right now? The way you've been stringing him along ..."

This is an honest-to-goodness nightmare. The room seems to tilt out of control until I find myself gripping the table in an attempt to keep from sliding around.

He's never liked me? He only used me to further his comeback?

"Excuse me, but I've had enough of this." I shoot up out of my chair before he can see me cry, and the legs scrape across the floor loudly enough to attract the attention of a few people around us. "If he asks where I went, you tell him I want to talk to him. But away from you. I never want to see you again."

"Don't worry about it." Todd snickers as I turn away. "You won't."

Chapter Nineteen

"I WILL KILL that guy for you. I swear to God." Hayley hands me another tissue, so I can blow my nose for the hundredth time since I arrived at her apartment.

It's a little late, and I'm sure she worked hard all day, but I had to go somewhere. I couldn't face going home and being alone.

And frankly, this is not the sort of story I want to share with Matt. I don't feel like hearing how he told me so, how he never trusted Dustin in the first place.

"You have to get in line because I would like to kill him myself." Then, I have to look at her for confirmation. "We're talking about his agent, right? Not Dustin."

"Maybe both of them—who knows? It all depends on whether or not that guy was telling the truth." She sits next to me, rubbing my knee while I wipe my eyes. "I'm sure it wouldn't be the first example of an agent stepping in and feeling like they have to protect their client. That could be all this is. Maybe he sees how close the two of you have gotten and doesn't like the idea of Dustin being involved with somebody so seriously while he's trying to make a comeback."

"But we aren't together seriously. That's the thing. That's what I don't understand. Why did he treat me the way he did back there? I don't want anything from Dustin. And I totally expect for him to forget all about me once he leaves the city."

"Did you say that to the guy?"

"Honestly, I didn't trust myself to try to say anything else without busting out crying. I had to get out of there. I can't imagine what Dustin thought when he got back out onstage and saw that I was gone." And I don't even want to get started on those women sitting nearby, what they must've thought of it.

"I'm sure there's an explanation for this. He wouldn't use you that way."

I want to believe her. I want so much to agree with her and to do it with all my heart. I want to believe in Dustin. I want to believe he's been so determined to pursue me because he sees something special in me. Because I, myself, am special.

"You have to admit, it's almost sketchy when you look at it from a different point of view." I sink back against the sofa cushions, wiping my eyes again. "You're looking at this as my best friend, and I love you. But let's think about it in another way. Why would he go out of his way to spend time with me? And I'm not fishing for compliments."

Her mouth snaps shut because she was about to tell me how wonderful and awesome I am, which is exactly why I shut her down before she had the chance.

"We haven't slept together—though we could have the other night, but that went south. I have nothing to offer him but someone who's willing to listen and understand him, and I figured that was enough. Between that and attraction, I thought that was enough to keep him interested in me. How naive could I have been? All along, he thought I was writing a book about him or that I would tell the world that he was the inspiration."

"And you think he was using you to boost his brand."

"Of course! Now that Todd put it like that, I can't imagine I ever saw this any other way. It makes total sense now. He probably even wrote that song about me, so I'd write about it in my book. I can't believe I was so stupid!" I have to bury my face in a pillow and scream; I'm so mad.

Hayley waits until I get that out of my system. "Again, wait until you talk to Dustin about it."

"What's he going to tell me? That Todd was wrong? That he was lying? Or even worse, that maybe they started out, knowing I was writing about him, and he agreed to treat me well and woo me, but now, he has real feelings? Please."

"It wouldn't be the first time in the world something like that has ever happened."

"In real life? Or in one of the books I've written? Because that sort of thing only happens in fiction. No, the more I think about it, the more obvious it all is."

She sighs, resting her head on my shoulder. "I wish there were something I could do or say to make it better. I only want you to be happy and feel good. But I guess there's only so much I can do right now."

"You were here for me when I needed you, and that means everything." Then, something occurs to me. "Hang on a second. I really hope this doesn't become an issue for you at your firm if this news gets out and there's trouble between one of your clients and your best friend."

She lifts her head with a gasp. "He only could've talked to my boss, and I did tell him at one point that you and his client's client were dating. And I might've mentioned you were writing a book about a rock star. Crap. Is this all my fault?"

The genuine anxiety written along the creases in her forehead make me sorry I ever mentioned it.

"No, nothing is your fault. You're not the one who decided to string me along for the sake of free publicity."

"Again, you're not sure that's the case. Todd can see things one way; Dustin could see them a totally different way. You just don't know until you talk to him."

I check the time. Almost midnight. "He should

be finished by now. He should've been finished almost an hour ago actually."

"Maybe there are people he needed to talk to after the show. Like music writers or whoever. Or maybe he's arguing with Todd because Todd told him about your conversation and Dustin's furious and freaking out and firing him."

I have to giggle at that. "If only I could be there to see that happen."

"I wish I could record that happening, so I can watch it again and again. He sounds like a real pig, that guy."

"He acted like one too. I mean, I get it. He's in this to make money and to make a name for his client. But he was so mean and cold. For all he knows, I caught feelings for Dustin, and he completely broke my heart."

"Have you? Did he?"

"No, and no. Trust me, that's not the problem here. It would be so much worse if that were the problem. I was smart this time, and I didn't let myself get wrapped up in him."

"Smart. Good for you. Because I would seriously, without a doubt, need to murder somebody if you were hurt any more than you already are."

"Just my pride, and we both know that's been hurt more than enough times for me to be used to it by now."

"It's still worth murder. Just sayin'."

"This is why I keep you in my life."

She tucks a piece of hair behind my ear. “And I keep you in my life because you need somebody to threaten to hurt people for you since I don’t think you have a single violent bone in your body. Sometimes, people need to be roughed up.”

“Oh, like you would actually throw a punch in my honor.”

“You don’t think I would? Sweetie, there aren’t many people in the world I’d throw down for. You’re at the top of the list. In fact, you are the list.”

She knows just what to say to make me feel better.

I’m smiling when I ask, “Even the great Dustin Grant? Would you throw a punch at him in defense of my honor?”

Her eyes take on a steely look, her chin jutting out. “Honestly? After what you just told me? Without flinching.”

“I thought I was supposed to take the time to ask him first before making any judgments.”

“If what that Todd idiot says is true, yes, I would gladly slap Dustin into tomorrow because you’re better than that. You’re not the girl who gets used for free publicity.”

She gets up from the sofa to pull the teakettle from the stove. The girl thinks of everything.

I hug one of her throw pillows while I wait for my tea. Her apartment is soothing, warmer and cozier than I would expect a cool, brilliant chick like her to live in. There are plenty of plants and flowers on the windowsills, lots of pillows and throw blankets around. Her sofa is so comfortable that I've fallen asleep on it in the middle of a conversation. Twice.

My arms wrap a little tighter around the pillow. "To think, I was so happy that he wrote a song for me. Now, I know he only did it to look like the big, romantic hero."

She comes back, carrying a tray with mugs and a teapot and even cookies. "Where is he? I want to go have a word with him right now."

"Why am I the one trying to convince you that we should take our time and wait for the full story?"

"I'm sorry." She shakes her fists in the air after leaving the tray on the coffee table, scowling. "The more I think about it, the angrier I get. Who does he think he is? Like anybody has cared about him in years."

This isn't the time to remind her how nerdy she acted when she met him, so I'll keep that to myself. For now anyway.

If she thinks I'll never bring it up at any point in the future, she has another thing coming.

When my phone rings, we both look at it like it's a hissing snake.

"Please, let me." She's already reaching for it.

And that's fine as far as I'm concerned. I'm not ready to hear his voice yet.

"Kitty's phone. This is Hayley speaking." She

might as well be answering the phone at the firm, very businesslike. I'm almost proud of her since I know how angry she is—the hand not holding the phone is clenched in a fist, for example. "Yes, she's here with me now. No. I'll have to ask her."

She turns to me, putting the phone against her chest. "Will you go to the hotel to talk to him?"

Part of me wants to say no. I want him to sweat a little. I want him to feel terrible. I want him to ask himself how hard this must be on me and how he can make it up to me.

But then I remind myself that he might not care at all. If Todd was telling the truth, Dustin doesn't care about me in the least. And if that's the case, then I at least want to have my say before I close my eyes for the night. I won't go to bed with this hanging over me with no answers.

Which is why I nod in agreement.

And immediately wonder whether or not this is the right thing to do.

Chapter Twenty

I'VE NEVER BEEN inside The Plaza before. Not even for tea. When I was young enough that it would've been a fun treat, getting dressed up and going for a very grown-up day, we didn't have the resources to spend money on frivolous things. Grandmother would've taken me, but she and my mother didn't see eye to eye on a lot of things.

And while I was never old enough to talk about this with her, I get the feeling Mom didn't want Grandmother showing me a life she and my dad couldn't afford to give me. Maybe she was afraid I would end up spoiled, that I would prefer spending time with my grandmother to spending time with my parents.

And who knows? If Grandmother had introduced me to this rarefied world from a young age, I might have become that person. I might've resented my parents for not being able to give me what she could. But who's to say?

All of this goes through my head in a flash as I step onto the elevator. Dustin told Hayley he would leave word at the front desk that I was coming up.

All I had to do was tell them my name, and they'd direct me to the elevator. Maybe they could've asked for identification, but I guess they have more important things to worry about than a has-been being accosted by a fan.

I'm not exactly feeling charitable toward Mr. Grant as I ride up to his floor, and the feeling doesn't improve as I walk down the hall and knock on his door.

He wastes no time, and when he greets me, it doesn't come as a surprise that he's holding a glass of whiskey in one hand. He's clearly had time to break into the minibar since returning from his show.

I don't know what I expected. Maybe an apology? Maybe for him to reach out and grab me and pull me to him? Maybe for him to swear that he had no idea what Todd was thinking and that he's been falling for me since we met?

I should really know better by now, shouldn't I?

"What the hell did you think you were doing, walking out on me like that?"

As if that's not bad enough, he turns and walks away, leaving me standing alone in the hallway. I decide to take this as an invitation to enter, so I do.

The suite is huge and beyond gorgeous, or I guess it would be if there weren't clothes and bags and boxes lying everywhere. Either he's been shopping recently and hasn't bothered to put anything away or he emptied out his closet the way

I sometimes do … and hasn't bothered to put anything away.

"Do they not have maid service in this hotel?"

There's a stack of dirty dishes on the kitchen counter and a slew of empty bottles, cups, and glasses lying around. Like he's ordered room service but never placed what was left of it outside the door, the way any normal person would.

"I don't like them coming in and going through my things. If you had any idea what it's like to live my life, you'd understand."

Wow. He's feeling incredibly conceited right now.

I follow him to the bedroom, where he's currently looking through what's left on the hangers in the open closet.

"I thought I came here, so we could talk." I'm standing in the doorway, watching him go through the row of shirts and jackets. "So far, you've gotten mad at me for leaving the show when I did. We haven't actually talked about anything."

"So, talk. After that, we'll go someplace. Wherever you want."

Meanwhile, he hasn't taken his head from the closet yet. I'm talking to his back.

"Hang on. Maybe I don't want to go anywhere with you right now. I thought you understood I'm upset, which is why I didn't even answer the phone when you called."

"Todd said you were pissed after he talked with

you." At least he pays me the compliment of looking at me over his shoulder, frowning. "I should know better than to let him talk to anybody. Unless he's working out a deal for me or something like that, he's useless."

"Did he happen to tell you what we were talking about?"

"Not really. He said you were getting mobbed by people and he got rid of them for you. And that you got pissed and left."

Well, that explains a few things.

"Could you please stop rifling through the closet and look at me for a second? Because he left out a whole lot of what happened between us, and I think you need to know about it."

He turns with a sigh, shrugging. "Okay. I'm looking at you. Which is more than I want to do right now because you embarrassed the hell out of me by leaving after I sang a song for you. I didn't have to do that. I didn't have to announce to everybody that I wrote that song for you."

"I'm sorry. Am I supposed to fall on my knees and weep for joy? You know what's funny? I might have—well, maybe I wouldn't have gone that far, but I would definitely have been proud and happy and honored. But it's too late for that now because I spoke with your agent and he told me why you've been spending time with me. Because you think I'm writing a book about you."

His face falls, but he recovers quickly. "He

must've been confused about something."

"I don't think so. He talked to Hayley's boss, who told him I'm writing a book about a rock musician. Which is true. I am. But not you. And I really wish you had come to me with this because we could've talked about it before now. How long have you known about this?"

"I told him about your friend when you told me about her. Almost three weeks ago—that night you brought her to the show."

"So, for almost three weeks—since just a few days after we first met—you've been thinking that I'm writing a book about you? Is that right?"

"Well, aren't you?"

God, he's wearing the goofiest smile right now. And what I hate the most about it is that I can't help but see the person I used to think I was madly in love with in that smile. Because it makes him look younger. I can almost fool myself into thinking he's the kid he used to be—and heck, for all I know, he might be. Maybe he never matured past that point. Maybe all the good qualities I've tried to ascribe to him were all in my head from the very beginning.

I might've told myself I separated fact from fiction, but it looks like I never really did. And I know there's nobody to blame for that but myself.

"I hate to burst your bubble, but no. There is some confusion here. I'm not writing about you, Dustin Grant. I'm writing about a fictional musician who's trying to rehab his image, and his publicist falls in love with him. And guess what. He actually falls in love with her for real. He doesn't write a song about her just so she'll include it in her book."

He rolls his eyes, blowing out an exasperated sigh that doesn't quite ring true. It's almost too dramatic. "That's not why I wrote the song."

"That's a load of bull, and I think we both know it." The more I talk, the angrier I get. It takes real effort to keep my voice at a normal volume for the sake of anyone who might pass in the hall. "You want to play the big, romantic hero. Todd basically told me so. This is all supposed to be for your image. Isn't it? This is going to boost your visibility and improve your brand. Do me a favor and don't lie to me."

It's like I might as well not have said any of that. He's still stuck on what I said before.

"So, you're not writing about me personally."

"Why would I even do that? Do you know all the legal problems tied up in something like that?"

He waves a dismissive hand, snorting. "I would sign anything you want me to sign. Whatever kind of contract your publisher wants. I would give complete permission to use my name and even real-life situations we've been through."

It's like we're not even on the same planet. My jaw drops as I struggle to keep up with his warped train of thought.

"But it's not about you! It never was! Yes, I admit, I needed to learn what it's like for somebody in your shoes. But if you don't think authors go around all the time, using the people in their real life for inspiration, you need a dose of reality. After the first night we met, I've only been in this for you. Because of you. Because I like you. Because I wanted to spend time with you and hear your music. Not for a book, which I could easily write without you. And definitely not because I wanted to tie my name to yours in any way."

He bursts out laughing, plopping down on the king-size bed. "Right. Like that's not a complete lie."

"It isn't!"

"You mean to tell me that you wouldn't get an increase in readership if readers knew you were writing about situations inspired by me? Like you wouldn't get a single boost from my fans hearing about that and picking up your book?"

Here's the thing: if he had approached this as an adult instead of a spoiled child, I would probably react a lot better to that comment.

But he's been nothing but nasty and dismissive, and he hasn't even bothered denying anything Todd said. As far as I'm concerned, niceness is off the table.

"Do you honestly think I'm so desperate for new readers that your name would be the key to unlock some new level of fame? Is that what you're telling me?"

I have to say, he looks genuinely stunned. His

eyes go wide, and his mouth falls open. Maybe it was the tone of my voice that did it; I didn't try to sound pleasant. In fact, I sounded disgusted. Which was exactly the effect I was going for.

"So, that's how you felt about me all along? Like I'm what? A loser? A has-been?"

"You know what, Dustin? I never once thought about you that way until now, right this very minute. Now that I take a look at you and really see you, I feel sorry for you. The only pull your name has comes from the past. If it wasn't for those days, you wouldn't be here right now. Trashing a beautiful hotel suite by being lazy and gross. And if it's true what Todd said and you have all these women falling all over you and wanting to get into your pants, you would've done better, screwing around with them and leaving me alone."

That gets a reaction, and I should've expected it.

"Who says I didn't screw around with them?"

That hurts. That hurts a lot. No, we were never seeing each other exclusively, and I should've guessed he was sleeping around during all those nights we weren't together. But he doesn't have to be so cruel about it.

"What?" he sneers. "You think I'm that pathetic? That I'd save myself for you? No, babe. You were a challenge. I wanted to prove to myself that I could get you because you made it so hard for me. But there's always somebody around, wanting to fuck a rock star. So, I give them what they want."

My God. How disgusting can he be? How did I not see it? Was he really trying that hard to cover up who he is inside?

"Well, I'm glad for you. And for them. I guess they lived their teenage fantasy. Congratulations. Maybe, one day, you'll grow up and figure out how empty that is."

His face hardens into a bitter, loathsome mask. "I hope you know that unless you agree to include my name somewhere in your promotions for this book, you don't have my permission to write it."

"I never asked for your permission to write it."

"Right. And you don't have it. So, that's that."

"You know, it's sad that you think that means anything. It doesn't. The book's only a few scenes away from being completed, and I intend to have it finished in the next day or two. And I never planned to include you in it by name, and I was never going to use you for the promotion. I don't use people that way. I'm not like you."

"You use people all right. You just don't see it." He's a little wobbly when he stands, which tells me that's not his first glass of whiskey. By now, I know better than to think it was. "You used me, so you could write a book, and now, you're going to profit off that book. I deserve part of that profit. If I don't get it, then I want payment in some other form."

"The fact that you think I would add in some way to your popularity is actually sad, Dustin."

"Why? You write sappy love stories for frustrated stay-at-home moms and lonely career women. Most of my fans fall in that age range now, so it only makes sense."

"You don't have the first idea what I write, so don't even pretend you do."

For some reason, that's what bothers me the most. It's not how quickly he turned from Dr. Jekyll to Mr. Hyde. It's not even finding out that he's been sleeping with various women throughout the course of our pseudo-relationship.

It's the fact that he thinks I'm a joke.

He! Thinks I'm a joke!

"You write romance. It's not exactly rocket science." He brushes past me on his way out of the room, headed for the minibar. "Let's just admit we're both going to get something out of this and move on, okay? I really do like you. I don't want to fight."

"It's a little too late for that. And if you liked me so much, you wouldn't sound so nasty. At this rate, you're lucky I don't want to write a book about you because you wouldn't want your fans to read it."

He lifts a shoulder. "Even bad press is good press."

"Oh, believe me, it would be deeply unflattering."

He slowly turns away from the bar. "Are you threatening me?"

"No. I'm not that sort of person. But what I am saying is, if you don't think my publisher is going to have a word or two to share with your lawyer, you can think again. This isn't their first rodeo. And if you think you can get by on the power of name recognition alone, I hate to tell you, but aside from a certain, very narrow demographic of people, you might as well not exist. Romance is a billion-dollar industry, on the other hand, and you already know how many best sellers I've written."

He waves me out, splashing whiskey on the floor. "Get out of here."

"Gladly." Then, as an afterthought, I turn back toward him. "And by the way? That song you wrote isn't all that good."

"I didn't even write it about you," he spits. "I wrote that song a year ago."

I should've known better.

I should've known better about a lot of things in fact. I don't know whether I want to cry or scream or throw something as I leave his room.

All I know is, I never want to see him or hear his name again. Not ever.

Chapter Twenty-One

"I'M SO SORRY." It's probably the seventh or maybe eighth time I've said that since Maggie called, but it doesn't seem like I could possibly say it enough. "Seriously, this is all my fault."

"Like I've told you already, this is nothing we haven't seen before."

"So, what's going to happen? What can I do about this?"

"You can finish the book," she says with her usual snappy attitude, very direct.

And because she's so no-nonsense, I can breathe. The weight on my shoulders and chest eases. I imagined her taking this out on me, blaming me for this, telling me I should have been smarter or more careful. The fact that she hasn't done that yet bolsters my confidence a little.

"Okay. I mean, I was already planning on doing that."

"Good. Full steam ahead. His lawyer can say whatever he likes. There's nothing in the book to identify him in any way, so he can claim all he wants that it's about him, and we can just as easily say it's not. And even if it were, there's nothing derogatory about him. Nothing to tarnish his image."

I have to laugh at that. "His image. Give me a break."

"Honestly, Kitty, I would've chosen someone a little higher up on the food chain if it were up to me."

Yep, she had to find some way to remind me how I'd messed up.

But here's the thing: I'm only doing this because she told me I had to if I wanted to keep getting published.

"I'm sorry. I lost my address book with the names and numbers of every popular musician in the world. What was I thinking?"

It takes a second for her to get it together. Understandable since that's the first time I've ever taken a tone with her. "Excuse me, I think you forget who you're talking to."

"You're right. I'm sorry. But how was I supposed to find a famous musician to date? The best I was ever going to do was somebody trying to stage a comeback."

"Perhaps, from now on, you should stick to normal people. Regular people. Firefighters, police officers, members of the military. People who aren't going to try to bleed us dry."

"I'll keep that in mind. Honestly, it's not worth the hassle. That entire lifestyle. I could never be part of it."

"But you are part of it—at least, somewhat. You aren't a nobody."

"That's the beauty of being a writer. Unless you're a complete superstar, you can enjoy a little bit of anonymity. I like my life the way it is."

"What a shame this isn't the plot of some feel-good movie of the week." Maggie laughs. "We could all sit back and say we've learned a lesson from this while stirring music swells in the background."

It wouldn't be a good idea to get snappy with her again since I called her just as soon as I got home last night and left the most rambling voice mail she'd probably ever received. It's not even noon, and she already has the situation under control.

She's difficult at times, and I never quite know how to read her, but Maggie's one of the best for a reason.

"And hey! If all else fails, we can always get Blake to take care of things."

Yes, she would have to remind me that I once dated the owner of the publishing house.

"Good-bye, Maggie. More writing to do and all that."

When the call's over, I slump in my chair with my eyes closed, saying every prayer of thanks I can come up with. I spent the night fearing the worst, which means I got almost no sleep.

And that's just fantastic since tonight's the Halloween party at Hayley's firm.

Frankly, I can't believe she'd expect me to show my face now. By now, I'm sure people have heard about the whole thing with Dustin since Todd wants lawyers to get involved. It's all too complicated and embarrassing.

After begging her to let me off the hook, she assured me that everyone knows how stupid those two are for thinking they'll get anything out of it. She promised we'll only hang out long enough to be seen since not showing up would make it look like I'm hiding and embarrassed.

Which I am, for heaven's sake, but she refuses to sympathize.

I don't get her sometimes. I was a devastated wreck last night—not because of any feelings for Dustin, but because of how deeply he'd wounded my pride. How he'd lied to me, pretended to be somebody he wasn't.

And she expects me to go out and have a good time tonight?

There's still work I need to get done before I can even think about going out. Namely, the writing of my happily ever after, the scene that opens the door for my hero and heroine to walk off into the sunset together.

Sappy love stories.

Ugh, he's in my head, the idiot! I need to push him out of the way, so I can do my work. My important, well-read work. Work people love. Work that means something.

The jerk. The creep. Couldn't he have at least waited until I wrote this scene before showing me his true colors? I might've been able to get through it without wanting to throw myself out the window. It's just that the entire time I've been writing these characters, I've imagined them as Dustin and me.

I think it was different this time than it was with the last two guys. This was intensely personal for me since Dustin had already meant something. He had for years. The others I had just met.

I was setting myself up for failure all along.

Still, the words eventually start to flow. And then they stop. And then I delete a paragraph but come up with something better. I slowly shape and polish the scene and plumb the depths of my soul to figure out how to describe what my heroine is feeling.

How would I feel if this were me? If things had gone right?

THE STRANGEST FEELING of the past and the present sliding together, connecting like two pieces of a puzzle, enveloped her as he took her in his arms and swore to love her for always. For the rest of his life. Because she was worth protecting, worth cherishing. She was worth the world to him.

Just like she had always wanted to be.

OKAY. NOT BAD. Maybe not great, not yet, but I'm getting there.

Just in time, too, since I have to get ready for that darn party. If ever there was a night I needed to sit at home and binge on chocolate, this would be that night. But no. I have to show my face at a party I didn't want to go to before one of the firm's clients threatened legal action against me.

It makes getting into my slinky dress that much less of a thrill.

An hour. She promised we'd stay for an hour.

There's a knock at the door around seven thirty. Hayley said she'd pick me up just before eight. For a moment, I wonder if it's Dustin. That he wants to make up or at least smooth things over.

But I'm not a complete idiot. It would never happen.

And it's not happening because Hayley's at the door.

Conspicuously un-costumed.

"Um, you're not dressed. Or made up. What's going on?"

She's wearing a sweater and jeans and carrying a backpack over one shoulder. Not exactly what I expected.

"Are you supposed to be a student? I don't get it."

"You'll never guess what happened." She comes in like a storm, setting her bag on the floor and whirling around to face me.

"You could try telling me."

"Guess who's providing entertainment at the party. On the yacht."

"No."

"Yes."

"You're kidding me!"

"I wish I were. But no. Dustin's the musician they hired for when people go out on the water. I mean, Dustin? What the hell is this all about? Why would anybody want to listen to him at the firm's Halloween party?"

"Maybe they want a good scare?"

Hayley bursts out laughing. "I guess so!"

I can't help it. I join in. We both crack up until tears roll down our cheeks and we have to lean on each other for support even though nothing that just happened is particularly funny.

Because I'm laughing at a man whose music I loved before last night. At least, I told myself I did. Now, I'm making jokes about it. Life is weird.

"Needless to say"—Hayley wipes the tears from her cheeks—"we're not going. I wouldn't go to that party now if you paid me—even though I'd love to push him off the yacht. The temptation would be too strong. I can't put myself in that sort of dire situation."

"Thank God for that. I'm going to go change out of this outfit real quick." I run into my room and yell back, "What do you have in mind?"

"An at-home girls' night. What do you think?"

I think she's the best friend I could ever ask for since she's not the type to stay at home. Especially not on Halloween.

"That sounds good to me. As long as you actually want to."

"Girl, I need to." So much so, I guess, that by the time I join her in the living room again, she's already wearing pajamas. "It's not every day I get a chance like this. I thought I was gonna have to spend the night in heels, fake smiling at people I see every day. Now, I get to be comfy and hang out with you."

Yeah, she's pretty much the best.

"There's nothing better than the feeling you get after you've canceled plans, is there?" I ask, sliding down onto the couch next to her.

"Well, actually, there is," she counters. "It's that feeling you get when your best friend comes prepared."

I squint my eyes at her, not following, but then she picks up her backpack and pulls out two bottles of wine.

"One for me and one for you," she says, screwing off the lid and handing me one. "We don't even need glasses."

"You never cease to amaze me, Hayley," I say sincerely.

"Well, who needs stupid boys anyway?"

"Uh, I do. You know, to write my books."

She clinks her bottle against mine and says, "To the next hottie then."

ABOUT THE AUTHOR

Jillian Dodd is a USA Today bestselling mother-daughter duo made up of Jill and Kenzie—two writers, one pen name, and a shared love for fun, binge-worthy YA romance.

With over fifty books and millions of happy readers, their stories range from small-town love in *That Boy* to glamorous adventures and swoony YA boarding school dramas in *The Keatyn Chronicles, London Prep, Spy Girl*, and beyond.

Jill lives in sunny Florida with her husband, while Kenzie lives in Scotland with her husband and family. When they're not writing across time zones, you'll find them planning their next adventure or dreaming up lovable stories readers can't put down.

Check out our books and swag at
www.jilliandodd.net

www.ingramcontent.com/pod-product-compliance
Lightning Source LLC
LaVergne TN
LVHW091142080826
845145LV00008B/2230